THE RETURN OF THE DI SIONE WIFE

BY

CAITLIN CREWS

MILLS BOON

First published in Great Britain 2016
By Mills & Boon, an imprint of HarperCollins*Publishers*
1 London Bridge Street, London, SE1 9GF

Large Print edition 2017

© 2016 Harlequin Books S.A.

Special thanks and acknowledgement go to Caitlin Crews
for her contribution to the The Billionaire's Legacy series.

ISBN: 978-0-263-07054-5

CHAPTER ONE

THE HAWAIIAN ISLAND of Maui was tropical and lush, exactly as advertised, which irritated Dario Di Sione the moment he stepped off his private jet and into its unwelcome embrace.

The press of the island humidity felt intimate, and Dario didn't do *intimate*. The thick air insinuated itself against his skin, making the faded jeans and expertly tailored jacket he'd worn on the long flight from New York City feel limp and too close as he strode across the tiny tarmac toward the Range Rover that waited there for him, as ordered. A gentle breeze carried the exotic scent of the island—deep green things in exultant growth and the rougher, deeper smell of sugarcane production from all those fields they'd flown over on the way in to land—playing across his face like so many unsolicited kisses.

It only annoyed him more. He was trying to conduct a business conversation, not indulge in sensory overload on a damned tarmac.

"Is the car waiting as promised?" his secretary, Marnie, asked through the top-of-the-line, brand-new smartphone he had clamped to his ear. He was a proud user of his company's highly coveted products. "I was very clear about the need for a sports utility vehicle. The road out to the Fuginawa estate is very rough, apparently, and—"

"I can handle rough road," Dario told her, trying to rein in his impatience. He didn't want to be here so soon after the major product launch his company had pulled off this past weekend— or at all, for that matter—but that wasn't his secretary's fault. It was his. He should never have allowed an old man's sentimentality to win out over his own hard-won rationality. This was the result. He was halfway across the planet— when he should have been in his office—surrounded by lazy palm trees and exotic smells, all to appease an elderly man's whims. "The Range Rover is fine. And here, as ordered."

Marnie moved on to the long list of calls and messages she'd fielded during his first absence from the office he'd actually been sleeping in these past few months, a flashback to the kind of stress he'd been under six years ago when he'd first started with ICE. Dario scowled as another sultry breeze licked over him. He didn't like flashbacks and he didn't like that breeze, either. It was fragrant and sensuous at once, moving through his hair like a caress and getting beneath the fine linen of the button-down shirt he wore. Like a woman's fingers trailing down the length of his abdomen, suggestive and mischievous.

He rolled his eyes at his own flight of fancy, then scraped a hand over his unshaven jaw, aware that he looked a little more disreputable than the CEO of a major computer company, currently the darling of the tech industry and the smitten public, probably should. And he was about as interested in the intimate touch of Hawaiian breezes as he was in being here in the first place. *Not at all.*

This entire trip was a waste of his time, he

thought as Marnie kept talking her way through the pile of messages and calls that needed his personal attention immediately, if not sooner. He ought to be back in his office in Manhattan today, handling all of this in person. Instead, he'd flown some ten hours down his grandfather's memory lane to appease the very worst kind of nostalgic sentiment. Giovanni had sold off his collection of beloved trinkets years ago and had talked about them endlessly throughout Dario's youth. Now, ninety-eight years old and facing down his impending death with his usual sense of theater and consequence, the old man wanted them all back.

They remind me of the love of my life, his grandfather had claimed when he'd asked Dario to buy back these earrings for him. From a reclusive Japanese billionaire on his remote estate in Hawaii.

In person.

Dario actually snorted at the memory as he threw his bag into the back of the Range Rover and shrugged out of his jacket, too. He didn't know how he'd managed not to do exactly that to his grandfather's face when the old man had summoned Dario to his side earlier this month and made his outlandish request. But who refused an old man what he'd claimed was his dying wish?

"Email me those specs, Marnie," he told his secretary before she could ask what that noise was. Bless that woman. She was infinitely more dependable than anyone else he knew, including every last member of his overly dramatic and periodically demanding family. He made a mental note to give her another richly deserved bonus, simply because she was *not* one of the pain-in-the-ass Di Siones he shared his blood with, if little else. "Give me a minute to switch to hands-free and then start rolling the calls."

He didn't wait for Marnie to respond. He rolled his sleeves up, hoping that would cut some of the tropical humidity. He dug out his earpiece and activated it, then climbed behind the wheel of the sparkling, brand-new Range Rover. He started it up, punching the address he needed into the GPS and heading out of the small airport as the first call came in.

But even as he listened to one of his vice presidents lay out a potentially tricky situation with the brand-new phone they'd just released over the weekend, he was thinking about his grandfather and the so-called lost love of his very long life.

Lost loves, in Dario's experience, were lost for a damned good reason. Usually because they hadn't been worthy of all that much love in the first place.

Or possibly—and this was his pet theory—because love was a great big lie people told themselves and everyone else to justify their own terrible and usually painfully dramatic behavior.

And lost loves certainly didn't need to be found again, once the truth about them came out the way it always did. Better to leave the past where it lay, so it could fester on its own without infecting the present, or so Dario had always believed.

It had been difficult not to share his thoughts on that with his grandfather when Giovanni had told Dario that same old mushy story about love and secrets and blah-blah-blah. He'd shared it in one form or another all his life. Then he'd sent Dario off on this idiotic errand that anyone—literally, anyone, including the overzealous recent college grads working in Dario's mailroom—could have performed. But then, Dario was used to biting his tongue when it came to the foolish emotions other people liked to pretend were perfectly reasonable. Reasonable and rational and more than that, *necessary*. Whatever.

There was never any point in saying so, he knew. Quite apart from the fact that Dario wasn't about to quarrel with the elderly grandfather who'd taken him and his siblings in after his parents had died, he'd also come to realize that the more he shared his opinion on subjects like these, the more people lined up to tell him how cynical he was. As if that was an indictment of his character, or should allow them to dismiss his opinion out of hand. Or as if it should be a matter of deep concern to him, that weird fetish he had for *realism*.

He'd stopped bothering years ago. Six years ago, in fact.

And the truth was, he cared so little either way

that it was easier to simply do as he was asked—
in this case, fly across the planet to buy back a
pair of earrings that could easily have been sent
by courier had there not been so much *sentiment*
attached to them, apparently—than to explain
why he thought the entire enterprise was ridiculous. He was vaguely aware that the old man
had been sending all the Di Sione siblings off
on these pointless quests for what he called his
Lost Mistresses, but Dario had been far too busy
with this latest product launch to pay that much
attention to round nine hundred and thirty-seven
of the Di Sione family melodrama.

Surely they'd had a lifetime's worth already.
He'd been sick of it at eight years old, when his
hedonistic and undependable parents had died
in a horrible, utterly avoidable car crash and the
paparazzi had descended upon them all like a
swarm. His feelings on the subject hadn't im-
proved much since.

There was a part of Dario—not hidden very
deeply, he could admit—that would have been
perfectly happy if he never heard from another
one of his relatives again. A part of him that

expected that, once the old man passed on, that would happen naturally enough. He was looking forward to it. He would retreat into his work, happily, the way he always did. God knew he had enough to do running ICE, the world's premier computer company if he said so himself, a position he'd won with his own hard work and determination. The way he'd won everything else that was his—everything that had lasted.

Besides, the only member of his family he'd ever truly loved had been his identical twin brother, Dante. Until Dante had smashed that into so much dust and regret, too. He couldn't deny that his brother's betrayal had hurt him— but it had also taught him that he was much better off surrounding himself with people he paid for their loyalty, not people who might or might not give it as it suited them.

Dario *really* didn't want to think about his twin. That was the trouble with any kind of involvement with his family. It led to precisely the thoughts he spent most of his time going out of his way to avoid.

He'd assumed that if he performed this task for

his grandfather the way the rest of his brothers and sisters were supposedly doing, they could all stop acting like any of what had happened six years ago and since was Dario's fault. Or as if he shared the blame for what had happened in some way, as he'd been the one to walk away from his marriage as well as his relationship with Dante. He hadn't exactly *asked* his brother to sleep with his wife during what had been one of the most stressful periods of his life. And he refused to accept that there was something wrong with him that he'd never forgiven either his brother or his wife for that, and never would.

They'd let him twist in the wind, the two of them. They'd let them think the tension between them was dislike, and Dario had believed it, too busy trying to sort out what to do with the company he and Dante had started and whether or not to merge with ICE, which Dario had thought was a good idea while Dante had opposed it. All that mess and tension and stress and sleepless-ness to discover that the two of them had been betraying him all along...

Here and now, in Hawaii of all places, Dario

thought the only thing wrong with him was that he was still paying any kind of attention to anything a member of the Di Sione family said, did or thought. That needed to stop.

"It *will* stop," he promised himself between calls, his voice a rasp in the Range Rover's quiet interior. "As soon as you hand the old man his damned earrings, you're done."

He drove through the business district of Kahului, then followed the calm-voiced GPS's directions away from the bustle of big-box stores and chain restaurants clustered near the airport toward the center of the island. He soon found himself on a highway that wound its way through the lush sugarcane fields, then up into the hills, where views even he had to admit were spectacular spread out before him. The Pacific Ocean gleamed in the summer sun with another island stretched out low in the distant water, green and gold. The old volcanic West Maui Mountains were covered in windmills, palm trees lined the highway and exuberant flowers in shockingly bright colors were everywhere, from the shrubs to the trees to the hedges.

Dario didn't take vacations, but if he did, he supposed this would be a decent place for it. As he waited for another call to connect, he tried to imagine what that would even look like. He'd never lounged anywhere in his life, poolside or beachside or otherwise. The last almost-vacation he'd taken had been an extreme sports weekend with one of Silicon Valley's innumerable millionaire genius types. But since he'd landed that particular genius and his cutting edge technology after they'd skydived down to a killer trail run in Colorado, en route to some class-V rapids, he didn't think that counted.

Even so, he certainly hadn't been lounging around that weekend out west, contemplating the breeze. He'd always worked. Maybe if he hadn't been working so hard six years ago, he'd have seen what was coming. Maybe he'd have seen the warning signs between his brother and his wife for what they were instead of naively assuming that neither one of them would do such a thing to him...

Why are you dwelling on this old, boring nonsense? He shook his head to clear it.

The road headed out along rocky cliffs that flirted with the ocean, then turned to packed red dirt, and Dario slowed down. He was listening to one of his engineers when his cell signal dropped out, and he sighed, scowling at the GPS display that showed he still had quite a distance left to go.

He didn't understand why anyone would live out here, this far from the rest of the world. He knew the current owner of his grandfather's earrings was the kind of wealthy man as well known for his eccentricities as the family fortune he'd augmented considerably throughout his lifetime, but this was taking things a little bit far. Surely a paved road wouldn't have gone amiss.

But then, Dario loved New York City. He liked to be where everything was happening, all the time. Where he could walk down streets as busy at 4:00 a.m. as they were at four in the afternoon. Where he could be anonymous on the street and then recognized instantly when he walked into a favorite restaurant. He didn't understand all this lonely quiet, no matter how pretty it was out here. He didn't get what it was *for*. It appeared to allow entirely too much room for maudlin contemplation.

Then again, his idea of relaxing was closing a new deal and bolstering his stock portfolio. Things he was very, very good at.

Dario passed a tiny little country store that was the only sign of civilization he'd seen in miles and continued down the dusty, winding, rutted track at the base of the looming mountain. There were old, intricate stone walls and stretches of green pasture to his left, climbing up the steep side of the mountain, and wilder-looking fields to his right that gave way to rocky cliffs each time the road wound its way around again.

He felt as if he was on a different planet.

"Only for you, old man," he muttered.

But this was the last time Dario planned to extend himself, even for Giovanni. He'd had enough family for one life.

Without any cell service he was left to his own dark thoughts, which Dario preferred to avoid at the best of times—the way he'd been doing for at least the last six years, thank you. He shut off the AC and lowered his windows, letting that same mysterious breeze fill the car. It smelled like sunshine and unfamiliar flowers. It danced over him, distracting him, seeming to fill him up from the inside.

Dario scowled at that nonsense and focused on the rough, decidedly rural landscape all around him instead. It was hard to believe he was in one of the foremost tourist destinations in all the world. This part of Maui was not the luxury-hotel, world-class golfing mecca he'd been led to expect had taken over the whole island—or hell, the entire state of Hawaii. This was all gnarled trees and wild, untamed countryside. He made his way along the foothills of the mountains toward rocky beaches strewn with smooth pebbles and sharp-edged volcanic rock. A small, proud little church drew itself up at the end of the world as if it alone held back the sea, and then Dario was climbing back up into the hills again to skirt this or that rocky, black stone cove.

Right about the time he ran out of patience, he finally found the gleaming entrance that marked his turn inward to the Fuginawa estate. At last.

He had a brief discussion with a disembodied guard over the intercom before the imposing iron gates swung open to admit him. This drive was not paved, either, but it was noticeably better tended than the previous road—which was called a highway even while it was made of little more than reddish dirt and grass. The estate's private lane meandered lazily from the cliff's edge over the water until it delivered him to a sweeping, landscaped circle behind an impressive house that rambled for what seemed like miles in both directions, commanding a stunning view out over the water and on toward the horizon.

Dario climbed out of the Range Rover, unable to keep himself from taking the kind of deep breath that let perhaps too much of all that dizzy sunshine into his lungs. Fog clung to the mountain above him, draping the hills in ribbons of smoke and navy, the mist seeming to dance a bit as he looked at it. It made it hard to keep hold of his impatience, but still, he managed it.

Pretty wasn't going to run his company for him, and no matter that the sun felt good on his face after the mad crush of the past few weeks and a long plane ride. He glanced at his watch to see that it had just come noon here, as his secretary had arranged with Fuginawa's representatives. There was no reason he couldn't get the damned earrings for his grandfather and get right back on his plane. He could be back in New York by the start of the business day tomorrow. He certainly didn't have to stay in this odd place any longer than necessary.

Dario raked a hand through his hair and followed the path down toward the impressive, faintly Asian-inspired front door, his own footsteps seeming unduly loud in all the quiet. Even the door itself opened soundlessly as he approached.

He was beckoned inside by a smiling member of staff, who then led him through the graciously appointed house. It was all high ceilings with silent fans to move the air about, and shockingly expensive, highly recognizable art on the walls. The inside spaces blended seamlessly into outside spaces with walls that rolled back to let in the air and light, making the house wide open to the elements in a manner Dario found…reck-less. Very nearly disturbing, especially given the priceless paintings on the walls—but what did he care? It wasn't his art at risk. It was only his time he was wasting here, nothing more. The staff member invited him to sit in one of the out-side areas, tucked beneath an overhang wrapped with blooming vines, offering sweeping views out toward the deep blue Pacific Ocean and the winding road he'd just driven up.

It was still so quiet Dario almost thought he could hear the ocean waves crashing into the rocky black shore down below, when he was sure that couldn't be possible this far up the side of the mountain. He thrust his hands into his pock-ets. If he'd had to traipse this far off the beaten path into what appeared to be the distant edge of the middle of nowhere, he supposed a view like this made it almost worth it.

Almost.

He heard a step on the stones behind him and turned, itching to get to the actual point of this absurd journey so he could get back to New York as quickly as possible. He wasn't a hobbit en route to Mount Doom, and no matter if that mountain above him was actually the side of a dormant volcanic crater. He was a very busy man who didn't have time to waste gazing at the view on the back end of the world—

But then Dario froze.

For a stunned moment he thought he was imagining her.

Because it couldn't be *her*.

Inky black hair that fell straight to her shoulders, as sleekly perfect as he remembered it. That lithe body, unmistakably gorgeous in the chic black maxidress she wore that nodded to the tropical climate as it poured all the way down her long, long legs to scrape the ground. And her face. *Her face.* That perfect oval with her dark eyes tipped up in the corners, her elegant cheekbones and that lush mouth of hers that still had the power to make his whole body tense in uncontrolled, unreasonable, *unacceptable* reaction.

He stared. He was a grown man, a powerful man by any measure, and he simply stood there and *stared*—as if she was as much a ghost as that damned Hawaiian wind that was still toying with him. As if she might blow away as easily.

But she didn't.

"Hello, Dare," she said with that same self-possessed, infuriating calm of hers he remembered too well, using the name only she had ever called him—the name only she had ever gotten away with calling him.

Only Anais.

His wife.

His treacherous, betraying cheat of a wife, who he'd never planned to lay eyes on again in this lifetime. And who he'd never quite gotten around to divorcing, either, because he'd liked the idea that she had to stay shackled to the man she'd betrayed so hideously six years ago, like he was an albatross wrapped tight around her slim, elegant neck.

Here, now, with her standing right there in front of him like a slap straight from his memory, that seemed less like an unforgivable oversight. And a whole lot more like a terrible mistake.

* * *

Anais Kiyoko had been dreading this moment for six years.

Dreading it, dreaming it. Same difference.

And still, nothing could have prepared her for this. For him. For Dario, her Dario, in the flesh.

Nothing ever had. She'd never seen him coming. Not when she'd met him on an otherwise ordinary winter afternoon, not when he'd turned into a stranger in the middle of their marriage, accused her of the worst betrayal and then left her. Never. Today, Anais thought, she'd take control. She wouldn't be blindsided by him again.

She just needed to recover from the sucker punch of seeing him again first. She'd assumed she never would.

"What the hell are you doing here?" he growled at her.

That same voice, rich and low, kicked at her, leaving a shower of sparks behind. It was definitely him. She'd expected him, of course, but some part of her hadn't thought he'd really show after all these years. After the way he'd left things. After all this cruel, deliberate silence.

But it was him. It was really, truly him.

Dario stood there before her on Mr. Fugina-wa's lanai, the rolling green pastures of the remote Kaupo district's countryside behind him, the ocean a bright blue far below, like something straight out of her fantasies. And despite her many fervent prayers over the years, time had not smacked him down the way she would have preferred.

The way she'd prayed it would, more than once.

He was not a troll. He was not disfigured by his own cold, black heart and his dark imaginings the way he richly deserved. He was not stooped with loss or rendered appropriately hideous by the things he'd done.

Quite the opposite.

Unfairly, Dario Di Sione was the most beautiful man she'd ever seen in her life. *Still.* He exuded that intense, brooding masculinity of his the way other, much less intriguing men smelled of aftershave or cologne. He wore the kind of seemingly casual jeans only very rich, very powerful men could make look like formal wear, and one of those whisper-soft shirts of his that clung to the glorious planes of his chest, the sleeves rolled up to show off his golden skin and the sheer strength of his forearms. She knew that behind the aviator sunglasses he wore, his eyes would still be blue enough to rival the Hawaiian sky all around him, always such a dizzying contrast with the black hair he wore a touch too long and what looked like a day or two's growth of beard on his perfect jaw.

Damn him.

And damn her for being just as susceptible to him as she'd always been. Despite everything.

"I asked you a question."

Anais blinked, trying to shove aside her wholly unwanted reaction to him. But her fingers dug into the leather folder she carried, and she didn't think she was fooling anyone. Least of all herself.

"I hope you didn't have any trouble finding the place," she said, as if this was a normal business meeting, the kind she carried out as Mr. Fuginawa's lawyer, his first line of defense and his preferred method of communication with the outside world, all the time. "The road is a little bit tricky."

Dario didn't move. And yet she felt as if he'd reached across the distance between them and snatched her up in his fist. She had to force herself to take a breath. To stop holding the last one in as if letting it out might hurt her.

Especially when he slid those sunglasses from his face and focused all that furious blue attention on her.

"Really, Anais?" His voice was as mocking and withering as it was harsh, but she didn't recoil at the sting of it. She was tougher now. She'd had to be, hadn't she? "That's how you want to play this?"

Anais didn't look away. "Should we pick up the conversation where we left off six years ago, Dare? Is that what you want? The fact you cut me off without a word back then suggests not."

"Was that a conversation?" His voice took on that same lethal edge she could see in the tense way he held himself, and it made her stomach ache. "I would have chosen an uglier word to describe the scene I walked in on."

"That's because your mind is a gutter," she replied, still trying to keep her voice cool and professional, despite the topic. "But I'm afraid that has nothing to do with me. It never did."

He laughed. Not the laughter she remembered from when they'd first met, when she'd been a third year at Columbia Law and Dario had been finishing his MBA. The laughter that had made the entire city of Manhattan seem to stand still around him, lost in that rough sound of pure male joy. This was not that. Not even close.

"I don't care enough to ask you what you mean by that." He looked around, his gaze as hard as that set to his jaw. "I came here for a pair of earrings, not to play Ghost of Christmas Past games with you. Can you help with that, Anais, or was this whole thing a setup so you could ambush me?"

By some miracle, her jaw didn't drop at that.

Because she realized he meant what he said. She could read it in every hard, belligerent line of his body and that bright blaze of temper in his gaze.

"You knew this meeting was with me," she

managed to make herself say, though she couldn't pretend she still sounded calm or in control. "We've been emailing for weeks."

"My secretary has been emailing for weeks," he corrected her. He shook his head, impatience etched across his features. "I've been busy with things that actually matter to me. And don't flatter yourself, please. If I'd known you were going to be here, I wouldn't be."

And his voice was precisely as cutting as she remembered it from that horrible day when he'd walked out of their marriage, and her life, without warning and without a backward glance.

As if no time had passed. As if nothing had changed.

As if he really did think she was the cheating whore she still couldn't quite believe he'd so easily, so quickly, so *utterly* accepted she was based on one easily explained and wholly innocent moment with his awful brother. Just as she couldn't believe he'd never stuck around for that explanation—or even a fight. He'd simply...left.

Which meant all her silly expectations about this meeting today were nothing more than the same foolish dreams she'd nurtured all this time, all the while pretending she'd gotten over him and his shocking betrayal. That maybe he regretted what he'd done. That maybe he'd finally put aside his pride. That maybe he'd come to his senses at last. It was bad enough that she'd entertained such fantasies. It told her all kinds of uncomfortable things about how pathetic she was, how desperate and sad.

But much worse than her own hurt feelings and obviously messed-up heart, it meant that he still had no idea.

He still didn't know about Damian.

He really had come all the way to this remote corner of Maui for a pair of earrings, not for her.

And certainly not for their son.

CHAPTER TWO

"HAVE YOU LAPSED into a coma?" Dario asked, the silk and menace in his voice hitting her like a lash and cutting deep. "Or is this remorse at last?"

And Anais hadn't entirely realized *how much hope* she'd allowed herself to feel in the weeks leading up to this meeting with him, after all these years of silence, until now. When he took it all away again.

She should have known better.

"Remorse?" she echoed. She moved farther out onto the lanai, dropping the leather folder on the table between them and ordering her legs to stay steady beneath her when they felt like one of the palm trees being buffeted this way and that by the relentless trade winds. "For what, exactly? Your extended temper tantrum six years ago? I have a lot of feelings about that actually, but re-morse isn't one of them."

Dario's mouth moved into a hard, cynical sort of smile that made her stomach clutch. She'd had no idea he could look like that. So etched through with bitterness. She told herself he de-served it, but still. It made her ache.

"It's good to know you're as shameless as ever," he said. "But why change? It got you what you wanted."

"Yes. How silly of me. You storming off into the ether was exactly what I wanted. It's like you read my mind."

"My mistake, of course. Maybe you were an-gling for a threesome? You must have read too many tabloids. You should have asked, Anais. I would have told you that I don't like sharing any-thing with anyone, least of all my twin brother."

"I see you're still hell-bent on being as insult-ing and disgusting as you were back then. What a happy reunion this is. I'm beginning to under-stand why it took six years."

After the way he'd treated her, after the way he'd acted as if she'd never existed in the first place—refusing all contact with her and barring her from entering his office or apartment building as if she was some kind of deranged stalker—she *couldn't believe* that, deep down, she still expected Dario to be a better man. Even now, some part of her was waiting for him to crack. To see reason. To stop this madness at last.

Anais told herself it was because of Damian. She wanted her son's father to be a good man at heart, even if that took some excavating, like any mother would. She wanted his father to be the man she'd once believed he was, when she'd been foolish enough to fall in love with him. Because that would be a good thing for *her child*, not for herself.

Or not entirely *for yourself*, whispered that voice inside of her that knew exactly how selfish she was.

But life wasn't about what she wanted. She'd learned that as a child in Paris, the pawn of two bitter parents who had never wanted her and had only wanted each other for that one night that had created her and thrown them together, like it or not. Life was about what she had. Like her cruel, flamboyantly unfaithful French father and the embittered Japanese mother whose name she'd taken when she'd turned eighteen because she'd been the lesser of two evils, those two things had never matched. It was high time she stopped imagining they ever would.

She tapped her fingers on the leather folder. "These are the contracts. Please sign them. Once you do, the earrings are yours, as promised."

"Are we back to doing business, Anais?" he asked softly. She didn't mistake that tone of his. She could hear the steel beneath it. "I might get whiplash."

She allowed herself a careless shrug and wished she actually felt even slightly at her ease. "Business appears to be the only thing you know how to do."

"Unlike all the things you know how to do, I imagine. Or should I ask my brother about that? He was always the more adventurous one."

Anais would never know how she managed to keep from screaming out loud at that—at the unfairness and the cruelty of it, from a man whom she'd once believed would never, ever, say the kinds of things to her that her parents had hurled at each other all her life. She felt a vicious red haze slam down over her, holding her tight, like a terrible fist. But somehow, she beat it back. She thought of Damian, her beautiful little boy, and stayed on her feet. She managed, somehow, to keep herself from screaming like some kind of banshee at this man she couldn't believe she'd married.

Not that he didn't deserve a little bit of banshee, the way he'd acted back then and was still acting now. Still, that didn't mean she had to give him the satisfaction of acting insane.

She met his condemning gaze with her own.

"I have nothing to be ashamed about," she told him. Icily. Distinctly. "I did not sleep with your brother. I don't care if Dante has spent the past six years telling you otherwise. I didn't. He's a liar."

"I wouldn't know what he is," Dario said with cool nonchalance. "I haven't spoken to him since I found him with you in my bedroom. Don't tell me you two lovebirds didn't make it. How heart-breaking for you both."

That shocked Anais in a way she'd have thought was impossible. The Di Sione twins she'd known had been inseparable. *Until you*, she reminded herself. *Dante hated you on sight.* She tried to blink it away.

"The fact you thought anything happened between us—and still think it, all these years later, to such an extent that you feel justified in hurling insults at me—says more about what a vile, dark little man you are than it could ever say about me."

Dario seemed almost amused by that. "I'm sure that's what you tell yourself. It must be comfortable there in your fantasy world. But the truth is the truth, no matter how many lies you pile on top of it. So many it looks like you've convinced yourself. Congratulations on that, but you haven't convinced me."

If he'd been thrown by her appearance here, he was over it now, clearly. This was the Dario she remembered. The stranger who had walked into their home that awful day and had inhabited the body of the husband she'd adored a whole lot more than she should have. This cruel, mocking man who looked at her and saw nothing but the worthless creature her parents had always told her she was. As if that twisted truth had merely been lurking there inside of her, waiting to come out, and after their wild year together, he'd finally seen what they'd always seen when they'd looked at her.

Dario had done a great many unforgivable things, many far worse than how he'd looked at her that day, but that had been the first. The shot over the bow that had changed everything. Anais found she still wasn't over it.

At all.

His lips thinned as he looked at her and he reached for the leather folder, pulling out the stack of documents. Then he acted as if she was another piece of furniture. He ignored her. He pulled out a chair and sat down, then proceeded to read through the dense, legal pages as if he was looking for further evidence of her trickery.

Anais thought sitting down with him at the table as if this was a normal, civilized meeting might actually break something inside of her, so she stood where she was instead. Calmly. Easily. On the outside, anyway. Letting the breeze toy with the ends of her hair as she stared out at the water and pretended she was somewhere else. Or that he was somebody else. Or that his being here didn't present her with a huge ethical dilemma.

She didn't want to tell him.

He didn't deserve to know.

What if he turned this cruelty, this viciousness, on his own son?

But even as she thought it, she knew she was trying to rationalize her dilemma away instead of addressing it head-on, the way she should. Because he kept hurting her feelings all these years later, not because she truly believed Dario would ever do anything to hurt a child.

Not telling him now would change everything. She recognized that. Up until today, the fact that Damian didn't know his father had been entirely Dario's own fault. He'd made sure Anais couldn't contact him, and she hadn't seen how taking out an advertisement in the papers—as her aunt had suggested one night after a few too many of Anais's tears and rants to the heedless walls—could help her child. By feeding Damian to the hungry tabloids? By making his life a circus? No, thank you. And she'd have eaten a burning hot coal before she'd have called Dante for any help, that manipulative bastard.

Dario had maintained his silence ever since that day back in New York. That wasn't her fault.

But letting him leave here today no wiser? That would be.

She felt her hands bunch into fists and couldn't quite make herself smooth them out again, even though she knew he'd see it. He could think what he liked, she told herself stoutly. He would, anyway.

"I have something to tell you," she said woodenly, forcing the words out past lips that felt like ice and keeping her eyes trained on the sea. The beautiful Hawaiian sea that didn't care about her troubles. The sea that washed them all away, or seemed to, if she stared at it long enough. The sea that had saved her once and could again, if she let it. Even from this.

Even from him. Again.

"I'm not interested."

"I don't really care if you're interested or not. This might come as a surprise to you, but there are some things in this world that are more important than your feelings of persecution."

He pushed back in his chair and looked up at her, and because he was Dario, he appeared in no way diminished by the fact that he had to look *up* to meet her gaze. Or by the fact she was standing over him, wearing three-inch wedges that made her nearly six feet tall. If anything, he appeared even more powerful than he had before.

She'd forgotten that. How easily he dominated whole rooms, whole cities, whole swathes of people, without even trying. How that beat in her like her own traitorous heart.

"I don't feel persecuted, Anais. I feel lucky." Dario even smiled, in that same sharp and bitter way that she worried might actually leave scars on both of them. Perhaps it already had. "It wakes me up at night, wondering what my life would be like if I hadn't caught the two of you when I did. How many more ways would you have tricked me while I was so wrapped up in my work? How much more of a fool would you have made of me right under my nose? What if I'd never caught on?" He shook his head and blew out a breath. "I should thank you for being dumb enough to take my own brother into our bed. It saved me a world of hurt."

It shouldn't still cause her pain. None of what he said was a surprise to her. She knew what he thought. What Dante had stood by and let him think. Dario hadn't bothered to ask *her*, his wife, to confirm or deny his suspicions. He'd walked into the house, seen Dante buttoning up a shirt in their bedroom and leaped to the worst possible conclusion. He'd believed the worst, instantly, and that was that.

And still, she felt that heaviness deep inside of her, a little too much like shame. As if she'd actually done something to make him think so little of her. As if she could have done something to prevent it. As if, despite everything, the things he'd done to her and the son he didn't know he had was somehow all her fault.

She didn't think she'd forgive him for that, either.

"I keep waiting for you to come to your senses, but you're not going to, are you?" she asked softly. Rhetorically, she was aware. "This is who you are. The Dario Di Sione I met and married was the make-believe version."

She'd believed in that made-up version, that was the trouble. Why did some part of her still wish that was the real Dario? She should know better by now, surely.

"Whatever you need to tell yourself." He signed the last page of each set of documents and then shoved the stack of them toward her. "Can I have the earrings now? Or are there more hoops to jump through?"

"No hoops." She did her part with the documents, slipping them back into the leather folder when she was finished. Then she reached into one of the deep pockets of her dress and pulled out the small jeweler's box. She cracked it open and set it down on the table between them, watching the way the light danced and gleamed on the precious stones, perfect white diamonds and gorgeous emeralds. "These are the earrings. Note the size of the emeralds and the delicate craftsmanship of the diamonds. They're extraordinary and unusual, and Mr. Fuginawa would not have let them go to anyone save your grandfather. He conveys his deepest respects, of course."

"They're earrings," Dario said bluntly. He snapped the box shut as he surged to his feet, then shoved it in his front pocket. "Whatever tiny bit of sentimentality I had was beaten out of me six years ago, Anais. Old earrings are just old earrings. They don't matter to anyone in the long run. My grandfather is a foolish old man who should be using his money to make his last days easier, not for this kind of nonsense."

Anais straightened her shoulders and told herself to spit it out. To get it over with. To do what was right because it was right.

Because none of this was about her. It was about Damian.

"I'm delighted to hear you're so unsentimental," she said, and her only possible defense was to keep her voice as ice cold as she could. To act like she was a glacier, the way she had as a girl, because feigned, icy indifference was the only way she could get her parents to leave her out of their daily target practice. So that was exactly what she did now. It was almost alarming, how easy it was to slip back into old patterns. "Maybe this conversation doesn't have to be as unpleasant as I feared it would be."

He didn't actually sneer. Not *quite*. "This conversation is already unpleasant."

"Then what I'm about to tell you is unlikely to improve it."

Anais held that harsh blue gaze of his. She reminded herself this was the right thing to do, no matter how it felt.

Be cold straight through, she told herself. *Feel nothing but ice until you become it.*

She didn't look away. "You have a son."

"I beg your pardon?"

Dario felt bolted to the stones beneath his feet. Pierced straight through. His heart stopped beating, then kicked at him hard, while his entire gut seemed to drop down to the ground and stay there.

And Anais only stood before him, as calm and unbothered and *untouched* as ever, damn her.

"You have a son." She didn't seem surprised she had to repeat that. "We do, I suppose. Biologically speaking. His name is Damian."

He didn't think he could breathe. "Tell me this is one of your jokes."

"Because I'm renowned for my stand-up routine?" she asked tartly, and he recognized that sharp tone. He remembered it. On some level, it was much better than *unbothered*—but he couldn't process that at the moment. "No. I'm not joking about my child."

He continued to stare at her, like an idiot, while his head spun. As if she'd anticipated that reaction—and of course she had, he told himself bitterly, because she'd known he was coming today, hadn't she?—she reached into the other pocket of that long, flowing dress and pulled out something. It took him a moment to understand it was a slightly bent photograph, and then she was sliding it onto the table before him.

Dario didn't want to look. Looking would be admitting…something. But he couldn't help himself.

A small boy with black hair and his mother's eyes laughed in the sunlight. He was kneeling on a beach, his little body sturdy and perfectly formed. Ten fingers covered in sand, stretched toward the camera. And aside from those eyes Dario knew all too well came straight from Anais, every other part of his face could have been lifted from the pictures Dario had seen of himself and Dante at the same age.

There had been exactly one other time in his life when he'd wanted to deny the truth in front of him this much. When he'd felt precisely this sleepless and out of his depth and furiously incapable of processing what was happening. And this, six years later, was worse. Much worse. The world went white around the edges. Or maybe he did.

"How?" he heard himself grit out, not looking at her. He didn't touch that photograph and he didn't trust himself to look at her. Every muscle in his body was so tense he thought he might rupture something where he stood. There was a storm building inside of him and he thought it might simply blow him to pieces right here— a thousand jagged, broken shards of him, until neither one of them was left standing.

It took him a minute to recognize that storm for what it was.

Fury.

Pure and undiluted and directed straight at this woman and her betrayal of him.

Again.

"I'm sure that if you think about it, you can figure out how," Anais was saying. He wouldn't call that tone of hers *amused*, exactly. It was far too crisp and pointed, and she still managed to sound so distant besides. That made it all worse. "I'll give you a hint. It wasn't a stork."

He was still reeling. Dario pushed back in the chair and onto his feet, leaving the photo where it sat as if it was poisonous. He raked his hair back with both hands, and then he got a hold of himself.

It was painful.

"And how," he asked, his voice rough and his

gaze probably a lot worse than that as he finally looked at her again, "do I know this is my child and not Dante's? We're identical. I can't even take a DNA test to find out the truth."

She stiffened as if he'd struck her. Then her dark eyes blazed—and damn him, he preferred that over the chilliness.

"Then I suppose it will have to remain a mystery," she threw at him. "What a shame. Damian and I will have to continue doing just fine without you, you incredible jackass."

He didn't process what was happening until she was almost through the great, open doorway that was the length of the pulled-back wall. That she had thrown that bomb at him and was now walking away as if it didn't matter.

"Where the hell are you going?" he demanded. "After dropping that kind of thing on me?"

Anais stopped walking, and the stiffness of her back told him that was a battle. She turned slowly. Very slowly. He thought she looked pale, and her lips were thin, and he didn't understand why he even noticed that. Why he cared at all.

You do not care about her, he snapped at himself. *You care about this lie she's telling.*

"I'm going to carry on with my life," she told him when she faced him fully, in that overly precise way of hers that indicated the raging temper inside of her. He remembered that, too. He could even see the faint hint of it in her eyes. "What did you expect me to do? Stand here and cry? Beg you to believe me? I've already been down that road. I'm well aware it's a dead end."

"Then why bother with this conversation at all?" he gritted out. "Unless you just wanted to throw a few grenades around. For fun."

That smile of hers was much too sharp. One more blade stuck deep in his gut, a match for all the rest.

"The only difference this conversation makes *to me* is that I no longer feel any sense of responsibility about the fact you're too much of a sulking child to have picked up the phone and found this out years ago." She leaned forward slightly, as if some unseen hand was keeping her from hurling herself at him, holding her back from attacking him with those fists he could see bunched up at her sides. "Thank you, Dario. Truly. I needed the reminder that you're absolutely useless. And, worse than that, cruel."

She turned to walk away again, and he should have let her. He should have cheered her on. He couldn't have a child. He *couldn't* have a child. Not him. He'd never wanted one, not after his own disastrous childhood, and he certainly didn't want to test that theory with the woman who had betrayed him so horribly with his own brother.

This can't be happening.

Maybe that was why he found himself across the patio without knowing he meant to move, wrapping his hand around her smooth upper arm to pull her back around to face him.

"Don't walk away from me."

And it was a mistake to have touched her. It was a terrible mistake, because touching her was what had caused all of this in the first place. His uncharacteristic loss of control when he'd first met her. His astonishing decision to marry her—and who cared if he'd lied to himself and told himself it was to secure her a visa to stay in New York? That wild, nearly ungovernable fury when he'd discovered her deceit. He knew better. It had all been about this.

This touch. Her skin. The wildfire he was horrified to realize still raged between them that easily, that unmistakably, even now.

"Take your hand off my arm," she snapped at him, her voice not quite as cool as it had been, and he was the little man she'd called him, wasn't he? Because he derived far more satisfaction from that than he should. "Now."

Dario hated the fact it was hard to let go of her. That he didn't want to do it. But he forced himself to release her and he took a perverse pleasure in the way she rubbed the place he'd touched her with her other hand, as if she could feel the same lick of fire that leaped in him, too.

Chemistry had never been their problem. Never that. It was only honesty and fidelity that had tripped them up, or her stunning lack of both, and he needed to remember that. He needed to remember that no matter what his body agitated for, wild and loud in his blood just now, he knew who she really was.

"You kept my child from me for all these years. *Six years*. Is that really what you're telling me?"

"Please spare me the sob story you're making up in your head," Anais bit out, jutting her chin out as he stood over her, and whatever shoes she was wearing put her almost exactly level with him. That mouth of hers, *right there*, and what the hell was the matter with him that he could think about something like that now?

Especially when she was talking to him as if *he* was the person at fault, when they both knew better.

"You refused to take my calls. You moved all of your things out of our home while I was at work. You barred me from your new apartment building and you instructed the security people in your office to call the police if I tried to get in—which I know, because they did."

He shouldn't have been fascinated by the spots of color that bloomed on her gorgeously high cheekbones, shouting out her temper in unmistakable red. It was as if her betrayal and the six years between them had never happened. The fact his body didn't care about any of that made that fury in him burn brighter. Colder. As if he was complicit in his own betrayal here.

Against his will, he remembered the confusion of those first days after he'd discovered Anais and Dante together. How the stress from the work decisions he'd had to make had fused with the terrible blow he'd suffered and had made him waver. He'd considered going back on his decision. He'd considered a thousand things in the even more sleepless nights that followed, just him and his bitterness and the messages he deleted unread and unheard from both his twin and his wife. There'd been a certain comfort in knowing that nothing could ever hurt him as much as they had then. He'd built his new life out of that certainty.

It had never occurred to him that he could have been wrong about that.

"My emails bounced back and you disconnected your cell phone number," Anais was saying. "I watched you rip up a letter I left on your car, unread, with my own eyes." She lifted her hands and then dropped them again as if what she really wanted was to use him as a punching bag. He almost wished she would. "So what exactly was I supposed to do? How was I supposed to tell you? I tried. But you were too busy licking your wounds and hiding yourself away behind all the wealth and privilege you could stack around you like stone walls. That's not my fault."

Dario concentrated on his temper as if it would save him. He had the sinking feeling it was the only thing here that could.

"You're talking about a child," he said very distinctly. "If you'd really wanted to tell me, you'd have found a way. This is just another game. You never run out of them, do you?"

"I told you today, the very first time I've seen you since you walked out on me," she said icily, but there was nothing cold in that furious gaze of hers. "There's no game." She shook her head when he started to speak. "I don't have to stand here and listen to this. Your feelings about the child you could have known all his life if you hadn't deliberately hidden yourself away aren't my problem. I didn't tell you because I want something from you. I told you because it was the right thing to do."

"Anais…"

"And now I'm leaving," she interrupted him, her dark eyes glittering with emotions he couldn't name. He shouldn't want to name them. He shouldn't believe they existed at all. "I don't really care what you do with this information. Go lick your self-inflicted wounds some more. Pretend you still don't know. Whatever lets you feed that persecution complex of yours, I'm sure you'll do it."

He couldn't bear it. There was that fury in him and something much darker and deeper and worse. Much, much worse. Raw and aching and terrible. She eyed him as if she was looking for something on his face, but then her gaze shuttered and she started to turn away again—and he really couldn't bear *that*.

So he did the only thing he could think of to do.

Maybe he wasn't *thinking* at all.

He reached out, slid his hand over her delicate neck to cup her nape and pull her close and then he took her mouth with his.

It was the same madness he remembered. That

same wild burn that sizzled through him, lighting him up and making him crazy, eating him alive. She still tasted sweet and perfect, the way she always had, as if no time at all had passed.

Dario moved closer, slid his hands onto the thick fall of her hair, then tugged her mouth into a better angle beneath his and kissed her deeper, harder.

And she kissed him back, the way he remembered she always, always had.

She met him, a tangle of tongues and need while the fire between them raged, and their whole history seemed to dance between them in the flames. It was as raw as it was hot, as greedy as it was painful, and Dario knew this was the worst idea he'd had in a long, long time.

But still he kissed her, over and over, as if he could glut himself on her. As if he could block out not only what she'd told him and all the accusations she'd thrown at him, but the six years since he'd touched anyone like this or let himself be touched in turn. He hadn't wanted anyone near him. He hadn't wanted anything that resembled intimacy, with anyone.

And yet here, now, with that damned soft breeze still dancing all over him, and Anais's perfect mouth hot and demanding beneath his, he couldn't seem to remember why that was.

She wrenched herself away. He heard the small sound of distress she made and he hated that it lodged itself in his chest, like one more bullet in this strange afternoon bristling with them. She stumbled back a step until her back hit the wall, and she stared at him.

She looked as shaken as he was. He hated that, too—the idea that she could actually be affected, that she might not be acting...

Of course she's acting. Everything about her is an act.

He hated everything about this. This wild, untamed place. That insidious breeze that was messing with his head and making him feel restless and edgy. Anais and her lies and her deception, six years ago and today, and the fact she was still the most beautiful woman he'd ever beheld only made it worse. He hated that he could taste her now. That he could *feel* her again, as if her perfect lips were some kind of brand and she'd marked him. Changed him.

And he hated that she'd made him feel again, when he'd tamped that down and shut it off in those tortured days following the end of their marriage. He hated that most of all.

"While we're on the topic," he said, not even sounding like himself, because that was what she did to him, *still*, "I want a divorce."

Dario wanted nothing more than to make her feel as ripped wide open as he did, to take all the hurt and the fury and that spinning in his head, that unacceptable need that still surged in him, and make her feel it, too.

So he grinned while he said it, to make sure she got his point. To make sure it was painful. And because it was true and there should be a record of it. "On the grounds of your infidelity, of course. With my brother as the named third party."

CHAPTER THREE

THE KNOCK ON the front door of Anais's little house in Kihei, a few blocks up the hill from the ocean in a strictly residential, tourist-free neighborhood, came after nine o'clock that same night.

Anais scowled at the door as if it had transformed into a snarling monster.

Her comfortable two-bedroom house was arranged in a breezy open plan. That meant she didn't have to get up from the living area's couch where she had files spread out on the coffee table before her to see that the figure standing on her front step and visible through the panes of clouded glass in the door could not possibly be her aunt or uncle or any of her friends.

He was too tall. Too solid. Too obviously *him*, and besides, that knock had been brusque and demanding, not anything like friendly.

She gritted her teeth and wished she hadn't changed into her comfortable evening-at-home clothes after she'd put Damian to bed hours ago. Yoga pants and a tank top didn't seem like adequate armor against Dario. Not here in her own home. Not when she could still feel his mouth against hers from earlier, the way he'd tasted her and tempted her and taken her over, leaving her with nothing but that fire she'd convinced herself over the past six years had been entirely in her imagination.

Her imagination was pretty vivid, it turned out. So vivid her breasts seemed to swell at the thought of him now, and she felt that deep, restless ache low in her belly that only Dario had ever brought out in her.

Anais got to her feet reluctantly. She threw a glance over her shoulder toward the half-closed door to Damian's room, but she knew her little boy could sleep through a rock concert. And she also knew enough about Dario to realize that if he'd tracked down her home address and shown up at this hour, he didn't plan to wander off quietly into the night simply because she hadn't answered his first knock.

He knocked again, louder, and she blew out a breath as she crossed the room. She smoothed a hand over her high ponytail and wished she really was the cool, practical woman she'd gotten so good at pretending she was. The kind who could take anything in stride, including the reappearance of her son's father on her doorstep. The kind who wouldn't spare a single thought for how she looked under the circumstances.

That woman does not exist, she told herself staunchly. *That woman is nothing but other women just like me, faking it.*

Then she steeled herself and wrenched open the door.

Dario stood there before her on the lower step, looking edgier and more dangerous than he had out on Mr. Fuginawa's lanai earlier in the day. It was dark now, a thick Hawaiian summer night that seemed to cling to the edges of things. It made Dario look as ruthless as he did powerful, somehow. He stared at her, unsmiling and intense, and she was unreasonably glad his hands were thrust deep in the pockets of his jeans. As if that made him safer when she knew better than that.

He should have looked disreputable, in jeans and an untucked shirt. Instead, he looked like a particularly gorgeous object lesson in wealthy young scions who also happened to be world-famous CEOs of major companies at such a relatively young age. Not that she'd followed his many corporate exploits on the internet, or anything.

Anais folded her arms and stood in her doorway. She did not invite him in. And she didn't particularly care if every last one of her neighbors on the small cul-de-sac was watching this scene from their windows right now. If anything, that gave her the courage she needed to handle this.

Like a glacier, she told herself. *You're cold to the core. Heat can't touch you, even his.*

"I don't recall inviting you over for a nightcap," she said coolly.

She'd invited him to go straight to hell, and she hadn't stuck around to see if he'd taken her up on that. She'd driven so fast down Mr. Fuginawa's drive and then back out the rustic Piilani Highway toward home that her car had bottomed out in the rutted road more than once.

It hadn't slowed her down at all.

"Is this impolite? I'd hate to be *impolite* in a situation like this." His voice was as thick and dark as the night all around him, and seemed to stick to her as if it was barbed. Anais felt goose bumps shiver over her bare arms and had to fight to keep herself from rubbing at them and giving herself away. "Maybe you can explain the etiquette of secret babies and hidden children to me. I'm not as familiar with it as you are. Obviously."

"What do you want?"

"You claimed you had my son. What do you think I want?"

"Damian is in bed, the way small children often are at this time of night." She made a *shooing* motion with one hand. "Go away."

"I want to see him."

Anais had to grit her teeth to keep from shouting loud enough to bring the entire island to her door. "You don't get to decide that, Dario. You can't show up here after being absent his entire life and spring yourself on him in the middle of the night."

"I knew you'd use him as a pawn. Why am I not surprised that you're precisely this shameless?"

"He is *five years old*. He wants a father more than you can possibly imagine. I'm not using him as a pawn. I'm *protecting* him."

"From me?" If possible, his face got even darker. She thought his arms tightened, as if he was clenching his hands into fists in his pockets. "What's that supposed to mean?"

Anais couldn't pretend to keep calm any longer. She couldn't stay cool and smooth and hard. And she didn't much care what he might make of that. She didn't care about *him*, to be honest. Not when it came to Damian's feelings. Not when Dario could crush her little boy so easily. And likely would.

"It means I know what you do to hearts." She hadn't meant to say that. She wished she'd bitten off her tongue instead, especially when he made that derisive sound that might as well have been a punch to the gut, the way it hit her.

"This is exactly the kind of crap I expected you to say and I don't have time for it. I'm not going to participate in whatever great melodrama you have planned here, Anais. I want to see the child." He shifted, as if it hurt him. Or as if maybe he wasn't as hard as he seemed, either—but it was dangerous to imagine such things. She'd already made that mistake six years ago, and look what had happened. "*My* child, or so you claim."

"Listen to me." She stepped forward, out of her doorway and onto the wide top step, not caring that it put her much too close to him again, even raised to his eye level. She shoved her finger in his face and she wished it was something more substantial, like a kitchen knife. "This is not about you. I understand that you must be feeling all kinds of things right now. I'm not particularly sympathetic, but I understand. Still, Damian doesn't know you. You've been missing in action his entire life. It doesn't benefit *him* in any way to be woken from a sound sleep so that a strange man can brood at him. And if it doesn't benefit him, it's not happening."

Her voice had gotten loud there. Or maybe it only felt that way, as if it echoed back from the gentle movement of the palm trees and the thick, dark night pressing in against them. And either way, Dario did nothing but study her, as if he was assessing her weaknesses and looking for evidence to use against her. He probably was. She only acted glacial in short, controlled bursts. She'd long suspected that the truth about Dario was that, deep down, he truly was nothing but a block of ice masquerading as a man.

She didn't know how long they stood there, with nothing but the tropical night between them and all around them, the breeze dancing over them as if it was playing tag with the moonlight.

Dario was the one to break the silence, his voice dark, yet calm. "Why did you bother to tell me about him if you were only going to keep him from me?"

If he could put on that calm act, she could, too. She made herself do it.

"I'm not keeping him from you. I'm simply

choosing not to wake him up so I can parade him in front of you right this very minute. They're not the same thing."

"You planned all of this, didn't you?" He sounded as if he was marveling at the very idea, but his blue gaze was frigid as it held hers. "You want to stab a knife in my ribs any way you can. This is revenge served cold, six years later, because I didn't stick around to play your deceitful little games with you."

Anais made herself breathe, even though her temper and her sense of injustice at the *unfairness* of all this roared inside of her. She didn't know how she kept herself from hauling off and slapping him. Only that whisper of something else deep inside her, that worried what she'd do if she touched him again because she doubted it would be as violent as he deserved, kept her from it.

That and the little boy who slept even now only a few yards behind her, completely unaware that his life had irrevocably changed today. That nothing could ever be the same, because now Dario knew that he existed. His father finally knew about him. That made everything different.

"I'm not going to do this with you," she gritted out when she could trust herself to speak. Not to scream at him as he deserved, but to speak the way *Damian* deserved his parents to speak to each other. If she'd learned nothing else from her own parents, it was that. "You're the one who made yourself unreachable for six years, not me. You don't get to show up here and throw your weight around because you've suddenly decided that there's something worth paying attention to in this life you walked away from so callously."

"So you are planning to use him as bait. There's the calculating, manipulative Anais I know."

"You can see him." And it was for her to know how much she wanted to tell him the opposite, purely out of the kind of spite she knew made her a truly terrible person, down deep inside where she tried hard to hide it. "But it will be on my schedule, not yours. I decide he's ready, not you. Do you understand me?" When he only glared at her, his face like stone, she continued.

"This isn't about your pride or your ego or your miserable existence, Dario. This is a little boy's life."

The air between them went flat and taut. Then electric.

Temper, history. Fury and need.

It seared through Anais, from her exposed arms all the way down to her bare feet. She saw the way Dario held himself, as if he was *this close* to putting his hands on her again, and what worried her was that she didn't know if she'd push him away or pull him closer. The trouble with Dario was that she didn't know herself at all when she was near him.

But he stepped back instead, and Anais had to confront the fact that she didn't feel any sense of relief at that, the way she should. She felt... disappointed.

You are sick, she told herself in no little despair.

He raked a hand through his black hair, making it look even messier against the jaw he still hadn't bothered to shave. She didn't understand how that could make him look more attractive, not less. Or why she couldn't seem to keep herself from noticing things like that at a time like this.

Or maybe she did understand, and hated herself for that, too.

Dario considered her for what seemed like days, and then he bit out the name of one of the grand luxury resorts further south on this side of the island in exclusive Wailea.

"Do you know it?"

"Of course I know it."

Not that she'd stayed there, of course. The prices were astronomical, even by exalted Maui resort standards. And she'd hardly had a lot of call to stay at luxury resorts in the past few years.

"That's where I'm staying." He studied her for a moment. "I'll expect you tomorrow evening at seven o'clock."

"I'm afraid I have a…"

"Cancel it, whatever it is." His full mouth thinned and the way his blue eyes glittered made her heart leap in her chest. It made her the liar he'd always claimed she was. "Don't make me hunt you down, Anais. You'll like it even less than I will."

And then he melted off into the night. She heard the sound of a car engine turning over in the street, outside her line of sight, but she couldn't seem to move. She stood there on her own front step for much too long, as off balance as if she was out at sea on a rickety boat, trying and failing to handle the swell.

He'd left her with nothing to do but furiously debate whether or not she planned to follow his peremptory orders.

Of course not, she told herself sharply, shaking herself out of whatever daze this was and walking back inside. It took a great deal more strength than it should have to keep from slamming the door shut, loud enough to bring the house down around her ears. *Who does he think he is to issue commands? You don't have to pay that man the slightest bit of attention!*

Anais returned to the couch and tried to get back to the work she'd been doing, the work she needed to get done tonight, but it was no use.

She was too…stirred up. Too uncertain and off balance, still.

He's Damian's father, a countering voice reminded her, as if she was likely to forget it. *You owe* Damian *this, not Dario. Hammering out some kind of solution here helps him, and that's what matters. It's the only thing that matters.*

Anais hardly slept that night.

She couldn't get comfortable in her own bed. She checked on Damian more times in the night than she had since he was a newborn and she'd been terrified he might stop breathing if she relaxed her panicked vigilance even a little bit. He'd been so tiny and fragile for such a massive, lifetime responsibility and the blinding shower of love she felt every time she looked at him. She'd come to the conclusion that maybe she was the one who'd stopped breathing during those first, overwhelming months.

She hadn't been entirely alone, thank God. Her elderly aunt and uncle had been the only bright spot in her family tree her whole life, and nothing had changed when Anais had come here to Maui with the shards of her marriage clinging to her like broken glass. They'd taken her in without question, the way they had back when she'd been a girl, desperate to escape her warring parents for a school holiday here, a summer there. When she'd finally admitted to them that she was pregnant, they'd taken that in stride, too. They'd helped her get on her feet and figure out a way forward as the single mother she'd never planned to become. And they'd been a steadfast, dependable presence in Damian's life since his first breath.

Compared to some women, Anais knew, she had it good.

She reminded herself of that the next morning, when Damian woke up in his holy terror mode, in the full fury of all his five short years. She got his things ready despite his protests, wrestled him into something resembling an appropriate outfit for school, then had to cajole and threaten and bribe him into the car for a miserable ride all the way to drop him off.

She released him to his school with a muttered apology for unleashing a Damian in his most unreasonable and mutinous state upon them. Then she went into her law office where she was a senior associate for the single named partner and disappeared behind the mountain of paperwork on her desk. She told herself that she had no idea if she planned to go and see Dario *as commanded*. She told herself that repeatedly. But when her aunt called in the afternoon and asked if Damian could have one of his sleepovers at their house the way he did from time to time, it seemed like a sign.

"A sign that you should use the night to catch up on work," she muttered to herself, scowling at her cell phone after she tossed it back down on the nearest case file. "Not gallivant about with the dangerous past."

It wasn't until she was back home that evening and finally able to clean up the evidence of Damian's morning tantrum that she started to rethink that stance. She imagined Dario had visions of some appropriate movie child in his head, all serene smiles and quiet playtime with noninvasive toys under someone else's cheerful supervision. That was a lovely daydream of a perfect little angel. She'd shared it herself before she'd become a mother. But it wasn't reality and it definitely wasn't her son.

She found she couldn't wait to tell Dario so—and even a guilty look at the stacks of files waiting for her on her coffee table failed to sway her. The man who she suspected had sheets of ice where his heart should have been couldn't possibly want a child, no matter what he might have said on her doorstep. Hadn't he said so a thousand times when they'd been together? There was no reason that should have changed in all the time since. And Damian deserved more than a father who would, sooner or later, begrudge his very existence.

Anais had lived that bleak, miserable life. She wouldn't condemn her own son to it. *She wouldn't.*

The front desk was expecting her when she finally made it through the last of the summer traffic down through bustling Kihei and into Wailea, then followed the unobtrusive signs into the parking area of the exclusive resort. A staff member announced that Mr. Di Sione was waiting for her in one of the resort's private, waterfront villas and proceeded to lead her there as if one or the other of them was visiting royalty.

Of course. Nothing but the best for Dario.

But if she was honest, wasn't that part of the reason she'd found him so fascinating? He'd been a shot of controlled recklessness. Bright color in the middle of her black-and-white life. He'd been raised wealthy and indulged, and then he and Dante had made their own, personal fortunes while they were still in college. It had meant neither one of them had to pay any attention to the kind of boundaries other people had no choice but to obey.

And Anais had been feral, more or less. She'd raised herself in the crossfire of her parents' endless wars, and she hadn't had the slightest idea how to have fun, or fall in love, or be silly for absolutely no reason—all the things Dario had taught her.

Taught her, then taken away, as if all those things belonged to him and had only ever been on loan to the likes of her.

Anais got more and more furious as she walked, following the diffident staff member across one of the most stunning hotel grounds on Maui as the sun dropped toward the water, all sweeping views juxtaposed with sleek, modern designs that somehow evoked ancient Hawaii in the gathering dark—not that any of it registered. The truth was, she was lucky. She'd been an attorney for years now in one of the most beautiful places in the world. She liked her job, her clients and the life she'd built here. Practicing law was comfortable and it allowed her to take care of Damian and help out her aunt and uncle, too, when she could.

She was damned proud of those things. This was the life she'd built all on her own. Her parents had stopped even the pretense of any obligations to her the day she'd turned eighteen. Her husband had abandoned her seven years later, right after she'd finally learned to trust him. Yes, her aunt and uncle helped her as best they could and that had been everything to her at times, but ultimately Anais had made herself *by* herself.

Anais had never had Dario's kind of money, however, and she never would. She'd spent a long time telling herself she was glad of that—

that it was all the money he and Dante had made while they were still in college that had ruined him, in the end. It had made him expect too much from the world and everyone in it, as if he could make everything he looked at what he wanted it to be, simply because he wanted it that way. It had also trained him to see the very worst in people, as they schemed to get close to him and use him for their own ends.

She'd been arrogant enough to think she was the antidote to that, but it had turned out that once a man was poisoned, that was how he stayed. Unless the man in question wanted something different for himself. Dario had pretended he had, but he hadn't.

In the end, he hadn't wanted anything he'd claimed he did. Particularly not Anais.

And for some reason the exquisite four-bedroom villa that would have been more than suitable for a king and the whole of his royal court seemed to press that fact deeper into her as she found herself knocking at his door, the staff member having long since melted away into the exultant, flowered shrubbery festooned with torches and dancing with real flames against the sunset.

She knocked with a wide-open hand, loudly and rudely, and of course Dario didn't rush to answer her. It gave her far too much time to stand there and think better of this. To wonder what she thought she might gain from acquiescing to his demands no matter what her reasons might have been.

And worse, what she stood to lose.

Nothing with Dario had ever been straightforward. They'd skipped regular dating altogether—having fallen hard into something far more intense neither one of them had dared name. Then they'd gotten married much too fast, each telling the other and maybe themselves it was a cool, rational decision based on Anais's immigration status as a French citizen instead of that insane fire that had consumed them both in bed. Dario had told her very little about his family, except that his twin was the only one he truly cared about at all—and yet Dante had been openly suspicious of her from the start. She'd tried to ignore that, too swept up in her first year of law practice and the head-spinning reality of her first lover who was also the husband she didn't dare admit she'd fallen head over heels in love with.

Maybe it wasn't surprising that it had taken exactly one year for it all to fall apart.

There was nothing good to be gained by poking her fingers into those old wounds, she told herself then, scowling at the villa's front door.

This is for Damian, she reminded herself. She chanted it a few times, just to make sure she was listening to her own words, and knocked again. Louder.

And this time Dario swung the door open and took her breath away.

It only made her that much more furious with him. She kept telling herself *that*, too, with even less success.

Dario wore nothing but a loose pair of linen trousers that hung low—*much too low*—on his lean hips and made it impossible to do anything but gape at that remarkable chest of his. She'd assured herself that he couldn't possibly be as good-looking as she remembered, as perfectly formed, like something that ought to have been carved from marble and propped up in a museum. She'd had six years to decide she'd built him up in her head.

She hadn't.

If anything, he was far, far better than she remembered, all flat planes of muscle and that ridged abdomen, smooth olive skin and a dusting of dark hair that arrowed down beneath those low-hanging, decadent trousers. Even his bare feet were gorgeous, big and inescapably male, and she hated everything about this.

Mostly, she hated that terrible yearning that ripped through her, tearing her wide open and making it impossible to lie to herself about it. She wanted him. She'd always wanted him. That connection between them had been everything to her, for a time.

There had never been anything as huge or powerful or all-consuming in all her life, until she'd held Damian for the first time in the hospital.

She'd been silly enough to think that connection was what had forged the true bond between them, back then. That their marriage had been conducted for all the practical reasons they'd agreed upon in their analytical way—for Anais's green card, because Dario had liked the idea of a lawyer in the immediate family to handle the company he and his brother ran, etc. It had all made such sense on paper.

But the truth of it, the truth of *them*, had been what happened in the fire that raged between them. Always. At the slightest touch. At the ways they tore each other apart and put each other back together, night after night. The things they talked about in the cold light of day were their cover, their pretense. The nights were their truth.

That was what she'd told herself. It was what she'd believed. What she'd *felt*, deep inside, in that cold place no one else had ever touched.

Until he'd smashed it all into a million little pieces when he'd walked away from her without a backward glance.

"I hope you didn't undress just for me," she said, smiling faintly at him as if she found his bare chest—truly, one of the great wonders of the world, to her way of thinking, and she hated that she still thought it—embarrassing. For him. "I wouldn't touch you again with a ten-foot pole covered in all your wealth and status. Look what happened the last time."

CHAPTER FOUR

"STARTING RIGHT IN with the lies?" Dario asked.

And because she hadn't let him into her house last night—which annoyed him a lot more than he cared to admit, and had gotten under his skin the more he'd thought about it—he blocked the doorway to his villa now. She could see how she liked it, and if there was a part of him that was ashamed at his own childishness, he ignored it.

He ignored a whole host of unfortunate truths, many of them making themselves known physically, as he gazed at her. "Touching me was never the issue, as I think we both know."

She looked at him as if she pitied him, which made him want to…do all kinds of things he wouldn't let himself do.

Yet.

"I was foolish and young back then," she said in that prim voice of hers that had always,

always, driven him crazy with lust and need. Today was no different, damn her. "I thought the package mattered a lot more than what was inside it. But people change."

"Selective memory isn't change. It's a lie you tell yourself."

"Happily, you don't know me well enough either way." She shrugged. If it bothered her that he hadn't stepped aside to let her in yet, she didn't show it. That, in turn, cranked up his irritation even higher. "I could have undergone a huge personal transformation. I could be lying through my teeth. Neither one has anything to do with the cold, hard fact of your paternity, does it?"

Dario had woken up at eight in the morning New York time, which was six hours earlier than here in this lost corner of the world. He'd spent a couple of hours on the phone and another hour or so on his laptop, and then he'd dealt with the restless anger beating at him by going for a very long run on a dark island road that wound down to beaches made of hard, black volcanic rock. He'd greeted his first Hawaiian sunrise with a swim in the shockingly warm sea, and then he'd come back to his villa and banged out a hundred furious laps in the significantly cooler pool, just to make sure he had a handle on himself.

Except he hadn't.

He'd spent the day on a series of calls and video chats with employees all over the world, and then he'd gone on a second, much harder run up into the hills, and even that hadn't done a damn thing.

Not when Anais appeared in front of him again.

She looked as effortlessly sexy as she always did, and he bitterly resented it. He resented *her*. She'd been beautiful yesterday on that remote estate. She'd been ridiculously appealing last night in nothing but a tank top and stretchy pants that had clung to every inch of her long, shapely legs. And today it was worse.

Much worse.

She'd put her hair up into one of those complicated, seemingly messy buns that he'd used to love to watch her create with her clever fingers and a series of pins she shoved into the masses of her silken hair seemingly at random. She wore a deceptively simple blouse in a soft cream color that made her skin seem to glow, tucked into a pencil skirt in a warm camel shade that should have been illegal, the way it clung to her lean curves and made her look even more feminine and alluring than she already was. Some animal part of him hated the fact she walked around like this. That anyone could see her. Even the delicate red shoes that clung to her feet and wrapped around her ankles annoyed him, sleek licks of flame that anyone could lust after the way he did—and likely had.

She looked elegant and cool and distressingly, achingly sexy. As untouchable as ever.

And Dario wanted nothing more than to dirty her up, the way he always had. The way he had from the moment he'd first seen her, looking like a faintly irritated librarian, prim and disapproving and ridiculously gorgeous in hushed Butler Library on the Columbia University campus, where he and Dante had been making entirely too much noise one winter afternoon. He couldn't remember what they'd been laughing

about, only that someone had shushed them—
and when he'd looked up, he'd seen Anais scowling at him from behind a pile of books.

He'd had the sudden and nearly overpower-
ing urge to mess her prim exterior up a little,
get under her skin, see how straitlaced she really was. He'd wanted to peel back her winter
layers and her offended expression and see what
kind of woman lurked beneath.

Something inside him, in that swirl of heat
that unfurled in his gut, had whispered he already knew.

He'd wanted to get inside her, badly. Right
then and there. That longing hadn't eased any,
then or now.

And he was aware that the urge had nothing
at all to do with the child she claimed was his,
and everything to do with the madness inside of
him that had already claimed him once.

"Be careful, brother," Dante had said with
great amusement when Dario had kept staring
at Anais in that library, until she blinked and
looked away, her cheeks flushing. "She'll eat
you alive."

Dario hadn't liked that. His easy relationship with his twin had never been quite the same after an incident with a woman they hadn't known they'd both been sleeping with at the same time when they were younger. They'd forgiven each other, if not the woman in question—but Dario hadn't quite trusted Dante in the same way as he had before. It had bled over into their business. Dario had been overwhelmed back then, fighting to figure out the future of the company in that year before they sold—and he hadn't felt that Dante had been willing to shoulder his half of the responsibility. It had made him want to punch his twin right there in the library for even looking at the same pretty girl in a way Dario didn't like. He'd shoved it aside then, but he hadn't forgotten it.

Later, when Anais had packed up her things and headed out and Dario had made to follow her and chance an "accidental" meeting, his brother had outright laughed at him.

"Don't blame me when she ruins your whole life," Dante had said. "Which I can pretty much guarantee she will."

"You have no idea what you're talking about." Dario had shrugged on his coat. He had *not* punched his twin. "It's like your own, personal perversion."

"A city full of women who would throw their panties at you if you smiled," Dante had murmured, shaking his head. "They have. And yet you want to chase the one who disliked you on sight. Maybe I'm not the perverted one."

Dario blinked now, astounded that the memories he normally kept locked away and inaccessible had taken him over like that. He wanted to think about his brother about as much as he wanted to think about his marriage. Meaning, he didn't. More blame he could lay at her feet, he thought furiously.

He turned back into the villa and walked toward the kitchen area, where the hotel staff had left him a selection of fine wines. He heard her close the door behind her and follow him, those high red heels loud against the smooth floors, and he poured them both a glass. Red for him. White for her. The way it had always been, back then.

And he didn't think he imagined the way she swallowed hard when he handed her glass to her, as if the memories were getting to her, too. He hoped they were as unwelcome as his were, and as uncomfortable.

"What is this?" she asked, but she didn't put her glass back down.

He crooked a brow. "Wine."

"You didn't think to dress, but you had different kinds of wine delivered? What a fascinating approach to a meeting. No wonder ICE is doing so well." She tipped her glass toward his chest. "Do you tantalize your investors and stockholders like this? Maybe put on a little cabaret number to seal the deal? Everything begins to make a lot more sense."

He bit back the insulting words that flooded his mouth, because that was no way to play this game. And Dario had always been very, very good at games. He won them without trying very hard. He'd spent all day in heated conversations with his lawyers discussing the different ways he could win this one, too. Decisively.

But it was amazing how different the game

looked to him when it was dressed like this, all womanly curves and that mouth of hers he could still taste against his.

That didn't exactly bode well for what he had to accomplish here. But Dario ignored that with the ruthlessness that had allowed him to come into ICE and change the company from the ground up over the course of the past six years. He'd made it his. That was what he did.

"How does this work?" His voice was low, smooth. Appropriate, for a change. He was trying to make it seem as if he'd had time to calm down. To get his temper and his emotions under control.

To accept that this woman had kept his child a secret from him for five years.

Five years.

He told that tiny voice inside of him that knew he'd blocked her every attempt at contact, that knew he'd made contacting him impossible, to be silent. The point wasn't what he might have done—he hadn't had all the information she had. The point was what she'd done, and hadn't done, when she'd been the only one who knew everything.

She took a sip of her wine, then smiled at him. Almost politely, as if they were cordial strangers at a cocktail party. "Because, presumably, I'm the expert on paternity issues?"

He eyed her a moment and reminded himself this was a game. That he needed to win it—and that meant controlling his temper. "Because you're the lawyer."

"How this works is, we talk," she said. She stood on the other side of the marble bar that separated the sleek kitchen from the expansive teak-and-glass living area and gazed back at him. And if she was even remotely chastened, he couldn't see it. "Rationally and reasonably, if we can manage it. We come to mutually acceptable arrangements."

Dario was contemplating how much he loathed the fact that she still seemed so unaffected by all of this—and particularly by him, if he was brutally honest—when she tilted her head to one side.

"Do you think you can handle that?"

That sweet tone of hers with all that bite beneath it was better. It told him exactly where they stood. On the same uneven ground.

"If he's mine…"

"If you say *if* one more time, this conversation is over. For good."

He wanted to ignore that, but something in the way she watched him just then made him think better of it. Would she really walk out on him? He didn't want to believe she could. And he *really* didn't want to investigate why he thought that.

"I don't know what you want from me, Anais," he said after a moment. "You can claim the moral high ground. You can tell yourself that the fact I blocked your access to me is the issue here. We could argue about that for years."

"I'd rather not."

"It doesn't change what I saw."

He saw something flash in her dark eyes then, he was sure of it.

"You saw a man walk out of your bedroom buttoning up a shirt."

"I saw *my brother* walking out of *my bedroom*

with *my wife*," he gritted out. He slammed his wineglass down on the counter, and he'd never know why it didn't shatter and send red wine and glass everywhere. "Shrugging his half-naked body into one of *my shirts.*"

It took him a long moment to realize that while she did nothing but glare at him, with that otherwise unreadable expression on her face, she was trembling. Fury? Shame? Anger at being called out on her unfaithful behavior all these years later? Something as complicated as what surged in him—as much desire as what he desperately hoped was distaste? He didn't know.

"Yes," she said, after a minute. "That's what you saw. You didn't see Dante and me naked and writhing around. You didn't even see us touching. You saw your brother changing his shirt, and you ended our marriage on the spot."

But Dario had been angrier with Dante by the day back then. Dario had walked in and seen what he'd seen and it had all made so much sense. That tension between Dante and Anais that Anais had assured him was *dislike*. The distance between the twins where their business was concerned, that Dante had claimed was about *different philosophies*. All such lies and misdirection. *This is the truth*, he'd thought then, like a death knell inside of him. All his late hours, all his work, all the responsibility he'd been carrying—it had all been a ruse, to keep him out of the way, so these two people who supposedly loved him and hated each other could meet. In his bedroom.

It still made him furious, as a matter of fact, when he should have been over it years ago.

He thought she could hear it in his voice when he spoke again. "Is this where you think I'm going to beg you to tell me what was really going on that day? So you can spin some fairy tale for me?"

"Or tell you the truth."

He didn't quite laugh. "That's never going to happen. Don't be so naive, Anais. Or do I mean self-absorbed?" Dario shook his head. And though it wasn't an entirely fair representation of what had happened, he continued. "Do you really believe you're the first woman Dante poached from me?"

She swallowed hard enough that he could see it, and it didn't help matters to focus on the delicate line of her throat and the sheer perfection of that collarbone he'd spent many a night exploring with his own mouth. It didn't help at all.

"Damian is your son," she said after a moment. "I'm not going to argue about it. You either believe that or you don't, and if you don't, there's no reason for us to bother talking to each other."

"Then what we need to talk about is what any parents in these situations talk about," he said casually, as if this was an academic discussion with no painful personal history behind it. And as if he hadn't spent entirely too long today on the phone with his own lawyers, running through various scenarios. "Visitation. Custody. Child support. The usual things."

He thought she stiffened at that, or her dark gaze sharpened, but she only placed her wineglass back on the counter with a sharp *clink* and then folded her hands in front of her.

"Before you go too far down any kind of legal road, you should probably know that your name isn't on Damian's birth certificate."

He hadn't known he had a son a day ago, and yet hearing her say that made Dario want to howl at the sky. Break his glass and every other one in the villa. He didn't know how he managed to keep himself from doing all of those things at once. How he sucked it all back in and tucked it away and managed to sound nothing but faintly icy when he responded.

"I beg your pardon?"

"If you'd like to claim paternity," she said calmly, though her gaze was hard, "you'll have to first prove it, and then, of course, pay all the back child support you owe me since his birth."

"How mercenary."

"Not at all. If you want to claim your son, you need to do something to make up for the fact you've ignored five years of his life. You can't go back in time and be less horrible to his mother, more's the pity, but you can pay. Maybe that's all you're good for, and that's okay." She smiled at him. It was not a nice smile. "Damian deserves a robust college fund out of this, if nothing else. It's not mercenary. It's an insurance policy."

"Other terms come to mind."

"You're filled with all kinds of unpleasant terms, aren't you?" She shrugged again. Dario was beginning to think that shrug might be the most infuriating gesture he'd ever seen. "That's not exactly a surprise."

"I never called you names, Anais, and I could have."

Her dark eyes glinted. "Don't sell yourself short, Dario. Your nonverbal communication was deafening."

"To be clear," he said when he could speak in an even tone, "you claim you're not using the child as a pawn, but you are perfectly prepared to hold him for ransom. Am I getting that right?"

"He's just a concept to you, Dare," she said after a moment, and he wondered if she knew she'd reverted to that nickname only she had ever used. He didn't let himself think too much about why *he'd* noticed. Especially when she was looking at him as if it hurt her to do so. "But to me? Damian is everything."

She shook her head at him as if she found him deeply lacking, and there wasn't a single reason in the world he should care what this woman thought of him. What her opinion of him was. Not a single, solitary reason.

More than that, he wasn't doing this to hash out things between them. He told himself he didn't care. This was about the child she'd hidden from him. That was the only reason he hadn't flown back to New York the moment he'd had those damned earrings in his possession.

He'd made a plan and he had every intention of carrying it out to the letter, and it didn't make one bit of difference what she thought of him or what she called him or anything of the sort. None of that mattered at all.

Why was he finding it so hard to remember?

Anais couldn't handle the way he looked at her then, so she turned away and walked toward the open doors that led out to his private lanai, with its gloriously unobstructed view of the sea and the fiery red sun sinking toward the distant horizon. He had his own beach if he wanted it, at the far end of a winding little path. She could see the white sand gleaming in the last of the daylight, and the waves rocked gently against the shore as if it was doing it for them alone.

And somehow, she managed to wrestle that great ache inside of her into something more compact as she stood there and gazed out at the water, the sunset. Something she could breathe through. Something that wouldn't betray her even further.

Dario was quiet for a long time, but she didn't turn back to see why. She felt him approach, though she wasn't sure she could actually hear him move, and then he was beside her, buttoning up a shirt made of the same lush linen as his trousers. It was also in black, and she didn't know what was worse. Him bare-chested before her like a thousand desserts she didn't dare touch, or him dressed like some kind of debonair lover, conjured straight up from the darkest part of the dreams she pretended she didn't have.

Both, maybe.

"I'm sorry," Dario said, and that was so shocking she whipped her head around to see if he was pulling her leg. But his moody blue gaze was focused on the sea, not on her. "I didn't mean for this conversation to descend to that level. That's not why I wanted you to come here."

"I imagine you wanted to beat me over the head a little bit with your might and glory," she said, her voice more bitter than she wanted it. More obviously affected. But she couldn't seem to control it the way she should. "This villa has to be at least five thousand dollars a night."

"Are you concerned about how I spend my money? I'm touched, truly."

"Only if it affects Damian." She made herself smile, as if this was an easy little talk. Or as if she was in some way light and airy herself. "That's the beginning and the end of everything, isn't it?"

She saw something move across his beautiful face, ruthless and determined, but then it was gone. She didn't think she'd imagined it, but she couldn't work out what his game was here, so she told herself it didn't matter either way.

"There's no need for us to fight, surely," he said, his voice low. Something like agreeable, which she found instantly alarming. "Six years is a long time. I don't see any reason why we can't have a calm discussion about what's best for Damian. We were rational once. Surely we can be again."

And that was exactly what Anais had told herself she wanted. That was more than she'd dreamed would ever be possible with Dario. So why was it she didn't quite believe him?

"I'd like that," she said. And then, despite that lingering sense that this wasn't real, she tried to be the generous person she thought she *ought* to be. The one she thought her son deserved. "I'd like Damian to get to know you, of course. But you do understand that he's an entire little person all his own, don't you? He came into this world on his own schedule and he's stubbornly stuck to it ever since. If you have some fantasy in your head about an angelic creature who will gaze at you and call you Daddy and serve as some kind of appendage to your whims, that's probably not Damian."

"It didn't occur to me that I would ever be a father until you told me I had a son yesterday," Dario said in a voice that sounded a little too close to grim for Anais's peace of mind. "I have no expectations that require modification."

She realized how close they were standing then, and worse, how obvious it would be if she leaped away from him the way she wanted. How he'd read into that and worse—how he'd be absolutely correct in what he read.

Anais didn't want to be so close to him she could feel the heat he generated, the way she did now, as if that black linen was a radiator even here in the tropics in August. She didn't trust herself.

Around Dario, she couldn't.

The sad truth was that she'd fallen in love with him a very long time ago. Not quite at first sight, but not long after, and nothing had changed that since. Not the way he'd broken the lonely heart she'd only ever shared with him. Not the way he'd abandoned her so cruelly, as if she'd been unworthy of a backward glance. Not the way she'd tried to hate him in all these years since, and failed, again and again.

How could she hate this man when she saw so much of him in her little boy's face? In that bigger than life laugh that was one hundred percent Dario in her son's body? It wasn't possible. She'd thought she'd come to a place of acceptance with that a long time ago. But of course, that had been when she'd never expected to see Dario again.

She still didn't want to stand this close to him. It made her entirely too aware of her own, eternal weakness where he was concerned.

"Great," she managed to say now, and she eased herself back and put a little more space between them, the better to look him in the eye, as if that would cut him down to size somehow. "Then when he throws a full-scale fit on the floor because he wants to wear a blue shirt instead of a red one the way he did this morning, I'm sure you'll handle it calmly."

Dario's mouth curved, and that wasn't helpful. It only reminded her all over again how susceptible she was to him. How badly some part of her wanted to believe that this—whatever this was—was real. God, how she wanted to believe that.

"If I can handle fractious board members and

morally dubious CEOs, one small child shouldn't be a problem."

"I'm glad you're so confident."

The air between them felt taut then. It shimmered like heat. Dario thrust his hands in his pockets in a way that suggested he wanted to do something else entirely with them, and Anais had to fight to conceal her delicious—and traitorous—shiver of reaction.

"I want you to come with me," he told her. "Let's eat a meal like civilized people. Let's talk to each other." That curve in his mouth deepened, and the truth was, Anais wasn't strong enough to resist him. She never had been. And just then, with all his deep blue attention trained on her, she couldn't remember a single reason why that should change. Why she'd want it to change. "Let's do this the right way."

CHAPTER FIVE

MUCH LATER THAT NIGHT, Anais pushed back from the table in the private corner of the resort's outdoor restaurant and tried, yet again, to caution herself. To go slow, to keep her perspective—*something*.

The night had been perfect. Anais was a local, yet she felt like some kind of princess tonight, immersed in old Hawaiian magic on all sides. They'd been whisked to this romantic corner of the hotel restaurant, where there was nothing between them and the sea but a strip of volcanic rock, any other diners lost in the darkness behind them. Torches danced in the thick air all around, and the breeze tugged strands of hair free from her easy chignon to slide over her cheeks like a lover's soft fingers.

But Anais had only ever had one lover, and

his fingers were hard, tapered and demanding, no matter how soft his caress.

The meal had been exquisite. The typical Hawaiian fusion of unexpected flavors and marvelous tastes, artfully arranged and beautifully presented, and Anais tried. She tried to sternly keep her attention on her son, not on his father. She tried to withstand the insidious magic of all this grace and ease and quietly luxurious wealth, and the man who had made it happen. She tried her best to keep her walls high, to read nothing into any of this, to stay the glacier she should have been no matter how enticing each bite of food.

No matter the far more worrying beguilement of the man across from her.

Dario had undergone some kind of transformation during the walk from his villa to the restaurant. Gone was that harsh, unforgiving man she'd met at the Fuginawa estate yesterday. In his place was, if not the man she'd married years ago exactly, certainly the closest thing to him she could imagine after these six long years apart.

And what the sound of Dario's laughter after

all this time didn't manage to do to her heart, the fine wine he kept pouring did to her head.

She regarded him from across the table now, watching the way the light from the flickering torch flames caressed his beautiful face and made him seem that much more like the many dreams she'd had all these lonely years. That much more the man she'd begun to think she'd made up from the start.

They'd talked about everything and nothing over their meal. She'd talked about Damian— who he was, funny things he did, the sort of stories that highlighted what a delightful little kid she thought he was, most of the time. Dario had talked about the work that clearly consumed his life, in a way that made it clear he was doing exactly what he should. He'd asked her about practicing law and how she enjoyed it all these years into it. She'd asked how he liked becoming so well-known in his own right, having nothing to do with his family. They talked as easily as they ever had, in and around all the submerged rocks and treacherous undercurrents that lurked between them, dancing over the surface of things instead of slamming into the obstacles.

It was all real enough, she supposed. Even... nice. It was lulling her into what she knew damn well was a false sense of security. What she didn't know was what she could do to make her traitorous heart pay attention to warning signs and potential alarms when all it saw—all it wanted to see—was the only man she'd ever loved here with her at last, treating her the way he had when she'd imagined he might love her back.

"Why are you doing this?" she asked softly.

"Eating dinner?" He leaned back in his own chair. "I try to do it at least once an evening. It's an odd personality quirk of mine."

"No." And it terrified her how much—how strongly—she didn't want to do this just then. How terribly she wanted to simply drift off into this fantasy world where there was nothing but faint Hawaiian music on the sweet night air and where Dario, still her husband, looked at her as if he'd never hated her and never could. As if the six years of separation had been the dream, not what had preceded it. "You know what I mean."

He didn't answer. He stood instead, smoothing a hand over the front of his soft black shirt, and Anais's heart sank. She'd ruined it, hadn't she? Would it have really mattered all that much if she'd let this keep on going for another few minutes? An hour? If she'd let herself bask in this no matter how much of a dream it was? Who would it have hurt?

But she already knew the answer to that question. Not Damian—she'd protect him with her last breath. Only her.

Only and ever her.

And yet there was something about the sweet night air that made her imagine she could take it. That a few stolen moments with Dario would be worth whatever pain followed.

Dario stood beside her chair and she braced herself for him to say something hideous and cutting, to slap them both back down to that place they'd been in earlier. His face looked harder than before, no trace of that laughter of his that still split the night open with its rough joy and was clearly where Damian's came from, but she made herself hold his gaze no matter how difficult it was. She owed herself at least that much.

His hard, beautiful mouth moved as if he meant to speak, but he didn't. Instead, he held out his hand.

And Anais knew better. Of course she knew better. She'd been a single mother all this time, while he'd been off building empires and never looking back at all to see what destruction he'd left in his wake. She could have recited the reasons why this—any more time spent with him, especially time spent *touching*—was a terrible idea the same way she could rattle off pertinent case law when necessary at work.

Here, now, none of that seemed to matter.

Nothing seemed to matter except the way he looked at her over his outstretched hand, as if he'd command her to take it if he could but was instead waiting for her to do what he wanted because, deep down, he knew she wanted it, too. She had the strangest feeling he knew exactly what battles she waged inside her head.

And worse, she thought he could see straight through her and deep into her chest, where her poor, battered heart felt swollen and broken at once, all over again—as if this was all something new, these things he conjured up in her.

Anais took a deep, shuddering breath, and then couldn't seem to keep herself from slipping her hand into his.

She didn't gasp out loud at the instant electric surge, at that hot touch as his hard fingers curled around hers, but she thought he felt the jolt of it as it seared through her. He tugged her to her feet and she went to him willingly, and for a moment they stood there with barely a whisper of the sultry summer air between them.

Her shoes were high enough to put her almost at eye level with him, and that made her veins thrum with something that was half music, half delight. His blue eyes looked much too dark, especially when they dropped to her mouth, and she felt that same wild current in him, too, lighting her up from the place their hands were clasped together.

Dario stepped back, though he kept hold of her

hand. There was a rueful curve to his mouth and a hard hunger in his gaze, and then he started to walk, pulling her along with him so she fit there at his side.

It took Anais much too long to realize they were weaving their way through the tables of the restaurant she'd forgotten was there. She felt as if she was walking through a dream, or as if the only real thing in the world was the way his fingers held hers tight and their palms touched. As if everything she'd ever felt about this man was boiled down into that tiny little touch, almost innocuous, and yet…not. At all.

The band kicked into a typical Elvis cover, syrupy and deeply Hawaiian, and Dario stopped walking when he reached the line of high palms that rustled there on the outskirts of the restaurant. The singer spoke of wise men and fools, and as Dario tugged her around to face him, Anais knew without a shadow of a doubt that she was very much the latter.

"I can't help it, either," he said in a low voice as he took her in his arms, and it took her a moment to realize he was responding to the famous song, not the words she didn't think she'd said out loud. "I've never been able to help myself when it came to you, Anais."

And it would have taken a far colder and harder woman than she was to pull away from him then. She didn't even try. Anais had never been the glacier she thought she should have been with him, not even all those years ago when she'd known she should have resisted him and hadn't. She wasn't sure she had it in her.

Certainly not when Dario was so close to her in the late-summer dark, his strong arms closing around her as he pulled her flush against him.

It was the middle of the night, she told herself, and she was pretending to be the kind of woman who had dinner with a man like him at all, much less at a stunning resort like this, and who cared if she'd actually married him in a different life? Those quick, painfully bright and deeply hurtful years seemed as if they'd happened to someone else. Surely nothing that happened in the lush dark here, on an island tucked away in the Pacific Ocean so many miles from anywhere, counted.

And she'd been alone so long. So deeply, profoundly alone. Before her marriage and after it. She'd been strong and she'd been brave. Too damned much of both, because she'd had to be to survive her childhood, her lonely early adulthood, the end of her marriage and her new role as Damian's mother and sole source of support. Her whole life had been a series of *had to be.*

Anais wasn't an idiot. This man had abandoned her. The likelihood was he'd do it again, probably before dawn. But she wasn't the naive creature she'd been back then, so shocked and destroyed when he'd turned on her, and the only good thing about that was that he wasn't likely to surprise her with that kind of betrayal a second time.

She didn't have to trust him to want him.

And she'd always wanted him. He was the only man who had ever touched her, the only man she'd ever let close to her, the only *person* she'd ever let inside. No matter how many dates her aunt and uncle and well-meaning friends had sent her on, no matter how many nice men had said nice things to her, no matter how many times she'd told herself that she wasn't *really* married despite the fact she also wasn't divorced—she'd never been able to bring herself to let another man close. She'd never let them know her at all, much less put their hands on her.

She missed it. She missed *him*.

He's still your husband, a dangerous voice inside of her whispered, as seductive as the whole of this long, perfect evening. *Whatever else happened between you, you loved him once. Maybe he loved you, too. Maybe nothing else matters but that.*

So she swayed closer to him and told herself it didn't matter what happened later. Tomorrow, two weeks from now, whenever. Nothing mattered but this. Here, now, where nobody could see them and no one would know.

She was so tired of being so alone. Maybe that made her weak. She decided she didn't care what it made her. Not when he could make it all go away.

He could. She knew he could. He'd made whole cities disappear with a laugh, the whole world with a kiss. He was far more magical than he deserved to be. She just wanted to taste a little of that oblivion again.

Hell, she'd earned it, hadn't she?

Anais reached up and wound her arms around Dario's neck, angling herself against him. His hands moved up and down the length of her spine in a lazy rhythm, tracing her. Relearning her. Sending a wild heat spiraling all through her until it pooled between her legs, a swollen, delirious ache.

And she was the one who lifted herself up and pressed her mouth to his.

She kissed him with all those dreams she'd kept pent up inside her across so many long years. She poured all the rants she'd aimed at her reflection instead of to him into it, all the tears and the fear and the loss. She kissed him with her broken heart and her new mother's terror. She kissed him and she kissed him, lonely and resolute, as strong as she was afraid, two sides of the same coin.

Finally, all these years later, she kissed Dario goodbye.

And he let her.

He slipped a hand around to the nape of her neck and he met her, as if he knew exactly what she was doing, what this was.

Anais was shaking. That might have been a tear that scraped its way down her cheek. She didn't care. This was a bloodletting. A ritual of loss and leaving, six years overdue.

And when she was finished, she pulled back, not exactly meaning to rest her forehead against his as she gasped for breath. But she didn't pull away when she realized she was doing it.

"Better?" he asked in a rough voice that hardly sounded like his.

It didn't occur to her to tell him anything but the truth, as if the Hawaiian night that brushed against her skin was its own kind of confessional. "No. Not really."

"Good." A small laugh, entirely male, snaked its way down her spine and made her shiver. "My turn."

And then he hauled her mouth back to his, and took control.

* * *

Dario should have felt triumph wash over him. He should have been wild with his victory, with a sense of accomplishment. He'd set out to seduce his errant wife and he'd done it.

But all he could concentrate on was the taste of her mouth beneath his, and better, the way she pressed her sweet body against his. Her breasts underneath that soft cream silk were like torture against his chest. Her arms were around his neck as she arched into him and it still wasn't close enough.

He couldn't get close enough no matter how he kissed her, and he couldn't pretend what he was feeling then had anything to do with revenge.

Dario shoved that unnerving truth aside and threw himself straight into the lightning storm instead.

He took her mouth with a ruthlessness that might have concerned him if he'd let himself consider it too closely, but he was lost in the storm. The electric burst of sensation between them. There was nothing but this slick perfection, the tangle of her tongue with his, the sensation of Anais in his arms again at last. It didn't matter why or how or what needed to happen next.

It only mattered that he possess her, totally. Now.

Forever, some traitorous part of him whispered.

Before he lost her all over again.

He didn't know how he managed to pull his mouth from hers when it was the last thing he wanted. He hardly heard the band as they rolled easily into another song. He barely knew where they were and he didn't much care. He only knew he needed her naked and that no matter how accommodating the resort had been so far, they'd likely take a dim view of it if he stripped her here and lost himself in her against the nearest palm tree.

Which meant they needed to go somewhere else.

Immediately.

Dario swept her up and into his arms without a second thought. He begrudged every step he took as he held her high against his chest and strode down the path toward his villa. Every second that he wasn't deep inside her, braced above her, wrapped around her the way he ought to be, was torture. The weight of her against him wasn't enough. The way she looped her arm around his neck was little more than a tease. The way she tipped back her head to watch him with that solemn expression that did nothing to hide the stark, unmistakable need in her gaze made the hunger inside of him threaten to take him to his knees.

It wasn't until he'd shouldered his way back into his villa, striding across the living room and into the sprawling master suite, that he faced the fact that he wasn't acting according to his hastily hammered out plan at all. This was no deliberate seduction, designed to tear her into a thousand pieces and leave her inert and destroyed and unable to lift a finger to stop what happened afterward. This was mutually assured destruction, and he had no idea what the hell he was doing.

He knew he should back off. Stop this right now. He set her down on her sleek red shoes at the foot of his platform bed and forced himself to let go of her. This was the perfect moment to rethink. Regroup. He wasn't in control here and that was unacceptable.

But he couldn't seem to care about that.

Because all these long years after he'd given up imagining any way it could ever happen again, Anais was standing there before him. Her smooth perfection was once again marred by his own hands, and he was so hard it bordered on pain. He reached over and dug his fingers into her thick, black hair, pulling on the bun so the pins scattered everywhere as it all tumbled down to swirl around her shoulders. Her lips were full and lush and faintly swollen from his. Her soft blouse looked crumpled against her breasts.

He still loved it as much as he always had. He was the only one who'd ever seen her like this…

No. A cold voice in his head stopped that line of thought. *Not the only one.*

And the fury that rose in him at that was nothing new, but the way it wound itself around all that need and hunger was. It rolled and twisted all over each other, becoming something new. Something darker and wilder.

He didn't want to think about it. He didn't want to reason it through.

He just wanted her.

God help him, but he'd never stopped wanting her.

As if she could read the turmoil inside of him like a book, a faint shadow moved over her lovely face and a line appeared between her brows.

"Dario?"

He didn't want to talk. He didn't know the difference anymore between his hunger and his fury, his sense of betrayal and his mounting need; he only knew that there was a single cure. He didn't want to think about the implications. He told himself that it didn't matter what he felt while this was happening, as long as in the end it achieved the desired result.

Dario had never believed that the ends justified the means—hadn't he learned that when he'd uncovered all the shifty practices his former silent partner in ICE had signed off on before he'd started there?—but here, now, there was no other way. He refused to allow himself even a moment of regret.

He realized he was staring holes through her when Anais shivered slightly, but the truth of things was the way her nipples poked hard against the soft silk of her top, telling him everything he needed to know about her own need. Her own hunger that had always matched his own. Dario concentrated on that now. He moved closer to her, indulging himself. He traced the stiff little peaks with his fingers, rubbing the silk against her own flesh and smiling slightly when she let out a moan.

Anais let her head fall back, and another beast roared in him then. Pure lust. Sheer desire. He stopped trying to pretend there was anything else inside of him—anything else that mattered. He buried one hand in the fall of her hair and got his lips on the line of her throat, tasting her. Testing the firmness of her skin. Reveling in the scent of her, as delicate and uniquely *her* as he remembered. With his free hand he tugged at her blouse, until he was forced to let go of her hair to tug it the rest of the way over her head.

Her arms were still up in the air when he put his mouth back on her, and he felt as well as heard the way she shuddered into him with a ragged sound. Her small, perfectly formed breasts were as exquisite as he remembered them, and he was delighted to find she still didn't bother with a bra. That meant it was as easy as a memory to hold her where he wanted her with his hands curved over her shoulder blades, and then to get his mouth on one dark-tipped breast.

Then he sucked. Hard.

Anais made a tiny noise that Dario hadn't realized had haunted him for years, that small sound of greed and yearning. And the taste of her was impossibly addicting, sweet musk and a hint of salt against his tongue. He moved his mouth to her other breast to be sure, using his tongue and the hint of his teeth until she was moaning out loud with her head thrown back, her hands gripping his biceps as if she wanted to leave her fingerprints behind on his skin.

He stepped back, then spun her around, so she was braced against the foot of the bed with her bottom in the air. She was still as beautifully formed as he remembered her, and he told himself that wasn't a stab of something like pain he felt. It wasn't loss. He focused on the silken line of her back, the indentation of her spine and the flare of her hips. He couldn't stand the obstacle of her skirt and reached over to unzip it, pulling it from her until it pooled at her feet and she was left in nothing but those wicked, cherry red shoes and a thong in the same bright color.

Dario thought he might explode right there.

Instead, he shrugged out of his shirt and kicked off his trousers, then moved behind her, reveling in the harsh sounds of her uneven breaths in the quiet room.

"What about my shoes?" she whispered when he smoothed his hands over her hips, as if he was trying to memorize them anew, imprint them into his palms.

"Leave them on," he muttered.

And he lost himself in her. He threw the past out of his head and he simply drowned in her the way he wanted to do. The feel of her warm, soft skin beneath his hands. The noises she made, tiny gasps and sweet moans, all leading to that critical point where her breathing became panting instead.

He flipped her over, then tossed her farther up the wide mattress and followed her down. He kissed her again. Deeper, wilder. And this time it didn't matter where they were. This time, he didn't have to stop.

Dario couldn't imagine there would ever be another night with her, not after what he planned to do tomorrow. And this wasn't like the last night he'd spent with her six years ago when he'd had no idea that she was betraying him or that it would be the last time he'd get to touch her. This time he was ready.

This time, he knew exactly what he'd be missing and how much it would hurt, loath as he was to admit it to himself.

So he kissed her like a drowning man, and when he couldn't take any more of it, he moved to lavish attention on her breasts again. And when she was writhing beneath him, her arms thrown over her head in abandon and her back arched high, he moved even lower.

He trailed fire over her belly, then moved over

that bright red thong at last. He pulled her long legs over his shoulders, then used his own width to keep her thighs apart. He liked the way she trembled, the way her breath sawed in and out of her and how she came up on her elbows to watch him.

Dario caught her gaze for a moment. If he didn't know better, he'd have believed that sheen of vulnerability in her dark eyes, that faint hint of emotion in her full lower lip. If he was still the fool he'd been, that might have ripped him apart. He could feel something hollow inside of him, as if it had.

But that was nothing more than another ghost, and there was no place here for that.

There was only tonight. There was only this.

Sex, he told himself harshly. *Nothing more.*

And then he pressed his mouth to the V between her legs, covered in that red lace, and made her call out his name.

She shook beneath him, the sharp heels of the high shoes digging at his back, and only when she made that high-pitched sound he liked too much did he tug the bright red thong aside, and lick his way into her heat at last.

He was like a storm.

Anais couldn't catch her breath, couldn't recover. Couldn't do a single thing in all the world but lose herself in the tumult and fire of Dario's wicked, masterful mouth against the part of her that ached so hot and needy she worried it might actually kill her. Or he would, and she doubted she'd mind.

He built up that fire, using his lips and tongue and the scrape of the jaw he still hadn't shaved. It was as if he'd plugged her into an electrical outlet. She hummed. She burned. She burst into flame again and again.

She dug her hands into his hair and held on while he licked her straight over the edge and into oblivion.

She'd almost forgotten the shattering. The sweet splintering. The monstrous ache that only Dario could ease, and the terrible need that only he brought out in her and only he ever assuaged.

And when she came back to herself he was already moving, tugging her thong from her legs and pulling her shoes from her feet, throwing one and then the next aside. She thought she heard them *thunk* against the hardwood floor, but then again, perhaps it was only her poor heart as it beat hard against the cage of her ribs and left her feeling a delicious sort of helpless as she tried to slow her breathing.

She couldn't seem to move. Or think. Or care too much about her inability to do either. One tremor chased another, leaving her boneless in the center of his bed. She heard the crinkle of foil that told her he was sheathing himself and then Dario was crawling over her, hauling her with him into the center of the bed before he propped himself above her on his elbows.

And for a searing moment, all he did was gaze down at her.

His face was drawn and his blue eyes glittered dark with the same passion she could feel sweeping through her, as bright as if she'd never broken apart beneath his talented mouth. As if he'd never thrown her over that cliff once already.

She moved then, lifting the hand that had once

worn his ring so proudly and placing it against his beautiful face. She didn't speak. She wasn't sure she could. She didn't know what on earth she'd say even if she could find the words.

Dario reached between them and positioned himself at her entrance, never shifting that intense blue gaze from hers. And then slowly, so slowly, he pushed himself inside her. Inch by glorious, impossible inch.

At last, she thought, *at last...*

Still he continued to slide himself into her as if he had all the time in the world to let her body accommodate him, for her channel to stretch to fit him. She couldn't help but remember their first time, when she'd been so scared and over-whelmed and in love with him. And he'd taken his time then, too. He'd built that wildfire be-tween them higher and higher, thrown her into bliss twice, before he'd moved to claim her com-pletely.

Just like now, he'd gone slow. So slow. So that his possession had felt inevitable. So that she'd shook beneath him, craving him, desperate to feel him sheathed inside her as far as he could go.

She didn't think she was the only one re-membering that faraway night, the two of them wrapped up in each other in his Manhattan bed-room with the whole great city a glittering flame outside his window. Anais had clung to him and welcomed him and found herself in him, and nothing had ever been the same after that.

So, too, would nothing be the same after this. But at least she knew that now. She wasn't that overawed virgin anymore. She knew exactly what she was doing.

If she kept telling herself that, maybe it would eventually be true.

Dario settled himself completely against her, stretching her. Anais could see the tension that corded his neck and made his arms like granite. She could see the mad glitter in his eyes that re-minded her of the whole of Manhattan outside that window in his old apartment, and she could feel him, bold and male and uncompromising, so deep inside her it was hard to tell which one of them was which.

As if it was her first time all over again, she felt moisture gather in the corners of her eyes.

And the way she had then, she moved her hips experimentally, to see if it made him blow out a breath the way it had before.

When it did, that mouth of his crooked up in the corner.

"This is no time for games, Anais," he told her in that gorgeously dark voice of his that swept through her like a new caress, setting her alight.

And only then did he begin to move.

He set a hard pace, and she met him. He dropped down to take her mouth again, slipping his hands beneath her bottom to lift her and hold her precisely where he wanted her as he thrust into her.

She clung to his shoulders and she wrapped her legs around his hips and she knew this dance. She knew precisely how they fit together, exactly how they moved. As if they'd been made for this. As if no time had passed.

And it took no time at all, or it took a lifetime, before Anais was strung out on that same high cliff all over again. She heard her own voice calling out wordless prayers into the dark, and she heard his low laugh, and then she was shattering all around him all over again.

And this time, he followed her over the edge—and she was sure she heard him shout her name as he fell.

CHAPTER SIX

ANAIS WOKE TO find the sun streaming across her face and the sound of the surf in her ears. She blinked in all the brightness and then sat up too quickly, taking in the vast room, the sleek furnishings, the astonishing softness of the dizzyingly high-thread-count sheets against her skin.

She wasn't particularly surprised to find herself alone. She wasn't necessarily happy about it, of course, but she couldn't claim she was *surprised*. No matter the places they could take each other in bed, out of it she and Dario seemed destined to do nothing but hurt each other.

Over and over again.

Anais moved very slowly, very carefully, to the edge of the bed and was faintly disappointed that nothing sang out in pain as she did. No twinges or tugs to remind her in that raw, physical way of how she'd spent most of the previous night, or with whom. Nothing that would last.

She told herself that was better. Memories were bad enough. They could lurk about for years, as she knew all too well. They snuck into the corners of things and blended into the shadows. They could ruin a woman without her even realizing it, popping up in dreams whenever she closed her eyes and making her unwilling to even consider moving on the way she should. No matter that *he* had, and years before.

But this was neither the place nor the time to worry about the ways Dario would likely haunt her now. Besides, she'd had six years to find a way to handle it before and she'd managed it. This would be no different. She'd be fine.

Eventually, she assured herself, *you'll be perfectly fine.*

Her clothes were draped over the chaise in the corner near the open glass doors, the screen letting in the ocean's song and the summer sunlight but none of Hawaii's less pleasant realities.

Reality is better, no matter how unpleasant, she told herself firmly as she dressed. *This*

place—Dario—it's all a fantasy that has noth-
ing to do with you or your actual life. It never
did. It all might as well be another dream.

That made her feel better—or at least ready
to face him. She raked her fingers through her
hair, letting it fall where it would and happy
that it conformed to its usual sleek, straight, de-
pressingly unchangeable style without her having to do anything more than that. She'd never
before realized how lucky she was to have such
hair that allowed her to look a lot more pulled
together than a woman wearing last night's outfit should.

She slipped her shoes back on as if they were
armor and she then squared her shoulders before she pushed through the door and marched
out into the vast living area prepared to do
battle—but it was empty.

That confused her. It seemed so unlike him.
She stood there for a moment, listening for the
usual sounds that indicated Dario was near—
the brusque clicking of the keys on his laptop,
the sound of his voice issuing orders on the

phone. But there was nothing. The villa was hushed. Still.

Empty, she thought. But she couldn't quite believe that.

There was what looked like a stack of papers on the kitchen counter, but she ignored it as she walked to each of the bedrooms and looked inside. Each was as beautifully decorated and as empty as the next. He wasn't in the little den with its massive flat-screen television, or in the separate office space equipped with a massive steel desk. He wasn't on the lanai or out on his secluded beach. He wasn't in the private pool on the far side of the villa, either.

He was gone.

Almost as if he'd never been here on Maui at all.

And Anais could admit it. It surprised her. And, more than that, felt a lot like a slap. The hurt feelings were silly, she recognized, but the other feeling bubbling up inside of her was a complicated sort of disappointment—as if she'd *wanted* what would likely have been another tense, unpleasant scene with Dario.

"Surely not," she murmured to herself, her voice the only sound in the villa.

She shook her head as she crossed the living area again, amazed at herself. At her own capacity for self-delusion and what amounted to self-harm. And she knew—*she knew*—there was a storm waiting there in the distance, bunched up on the horizon, dark and menacing. Thunder rolled deep inside her and the skies were threatening and low, but she was ignoring all of it. She was refusing to play through the images in her head of last night's abandon.

The way he'd touched her, the ways she'd tasted him—*no*.

She was pretending everything was fine—that *she* was fine. She was pretending that she could handle what she'd done last night and the fact he'd disappeared this morning, even though she'd half expected he would. She was desperately pretending she couldn't feel that cold harbinger wind on her skin, making every hair on her body stand on end, letting her know in no uncertain terms that there was no outrunning the storm—the terrible reckoning for all her reck-lessness—that was headed straight for her.

But maybe she could delay it awhile. Just a little while.

At the kitchen counter, she picked up the bag she'd forgotten she'd even brought with her last night and pulled out her car keys. And she couldn't help but glance over at the stack of papers, which it took her a beat or two longer than it should have to realize was actually a legal document.

With her name on it.

Her stomach flipped over, then plummeted straight down to her feet.

She reached over and pulled the papers toward her, and felt something like frozen solid as she scanned the first page. Once. Twice. It was only the third attempt that she was able to really, truly comprehend that she was looking at divorce papers.

Divorce papers for her and Dario, to be precise.

All drawn up and ready for her signature, demanding the divorce on the grounds of Anais's infidelity and naming his brother Dante as her lover. Just as he'd promised before in what she'd truly believed was simply a hateful, throwaway comment.

It took her another long moment to realize she was shaking. That the words were blurring there before her on the page.

There was a single sticky note attached to the last page, where the line for her signature sat, blank and cruel, next to the bold dash of Dario's name in an offensively bright blue shade of ink. The shiny yellow note contained nothing but a phone number with a New York City area code.

Dario's, she was certain. Not that she could understand why he'd left her divorce papers and his phone number. It didn't make any sense.

That terrible storm drew closer, the thunder growling ferociously at her as it came. She could feel the leading edge of the rain, battering at her where she stood...

Her phone began to ring in her bag, forcing her to breathe. To look away from the papers and that damned phone number. To shove back that storm as best she could. She tried to gather herself as she rummaged in her bag, and she'd at least taken a few calming breaths by the time she pulled out her smartphone to see her aunt's number on the screen.

"*Bonjour*, Tante," she murmured as she answered it, trying to sound calm. Normal. In one piece.

"Is Damian with you?" her aunt demanded in panicked French, without bothering to greet Anais at all, which could not have been more unlike her.

And Anais forgot about storms and papers and everything else.

"What? Damian? No—"

"The school just called," her aunt told her, her voice a streak of high-pitched upset, hardly intelligible. "I don't know how to tell you this, but he's gone. He went out with the other children for their midmorning recess and he never came back in. They're going to call the police, but I said I'd check with you—"

And that was when she understood. The harsh truth fell through her like a guillotine, swift and gleaming and lethal.

Dario's change in behavior last night. The abrupt switch from antagonist to lover. His absence this morning, the divorce papers, the damned phone number.

He'd planned the whole thing.

Including and especially her sensual surrender to him in bed, not once or even twice, but three times before she'd dropped off into an exhausted, dreamless sleep in the blue light before dawn.

"No, Tante," she managed to say. She would never know how she managed to keep herself from breaking down, right there on the phone. "Tell them not to call the police. Tell them it's fine. I know where he is."

"But, Anais—"

"I'll explain everything when I get home," she managed to grit out, and that wasn't a lie. Not exactly. Though she had no idea where she'd start.

She ended the call with her aunt and yanked the divorce papers toward her, flipping through the pages with numb fingers until she reached the signatures and that scrawled taunt of a phone number. It took her two tries to enter it correctly because her hands shook so badly and her thumbs seemed suddenly twice their previous size.

It rang. Endlessly. Anais thought she aged a thousand years before she heard the line connect and then Dario's smooth, calm voice, as effective as a gut punch. She doubled over, right there at the counter.

"Anais."

"Where is he?" Her voice was rough. Terrible. "What did you do?"

"He's perfectly fine," Dario said coolly. "He's happily watching a movie on his tablet."

"I told you I'd let you see him, you bastard. You didn't have to take him during recess! The school were going to call the police until they realized you were his father!"

"Go ahead," Dario invited her, and he didn't sound particularly cool any longer. "My son and I will be in New York in approximately ten hours. My entire legal team looks forward to handling the issue, however you choose to address it."

She couldn't make her trained legal brain work the way it should. She couldn't *think*.

"Dario, you can't—"

"I can and I did." His voice was the harshest she'd ever heard it. Worse than a stranger's, judgmental and cruel. "You never should have hidden my child from me, Anais. You reap what you sow."

And then, impossibly, he disconnected the call.

The smartphone fell from her hand and clattered against the hard marble, but she was already racing around the counter to pitch herself against the sunken sink and lose the contents of her stomach right there. Once. Again.

For a moment she thought her knees would give out. She could see herself in her head, sliding to the floor in a kind of puddle of despair and staying there until the hotel's housekeeping team swept her out with the trash. Her breath came hard and harsh, loud against the sink's hard walls.

But her knees didn't give out, somehow. Slowly, surely, she straightened. She braced herself against the sides of the sink and then she ran the water cold. She splashed it on her face and rinsed her mouth and slowly, slowly fought back the panic so she could think this through.

Dario wouldn't hurt Damian. That was the most important thing. He might be a terrible bastard to her, but he wasn't a monster. The worst-case scenario was that her baby might be scared, might want her and not be able to find her—she let out a ragged sob at that thought—but Dario had nothing but stacks of money at his disposal. Damian's physical and material needs would be met, no question.

She tried to take a moment to feel thankful for that. To remind herself how many women—many of whom she'd had as clients as part of her pro bono work on the islands—couldn't allow themselves that same confidence in their exes.

But the thought of her little boy afraid, however well Dario might treat him, made her shake again. She fought it back, and that dizzy, swimming thing in her head that was so much worse than a mere sob…she thought it might take her to the ground, after all.

But it didn't. She didn't let it.

She'd been prepared to do what she could to ease Dario's access to Damian. She'd wanted her son to have his father in his life, no matter her complicated feelings about that father. Despite what he'd thought, she'd never wanted to conceal Damian from him in the first place. She shouldn't have slept with him, certainly, but that was a minor misstep, all things considered. She wasn't sure she'd have forgiven herself for succumbing to that old addiction so easily, but she'd have handled it, somehow. She still would have done what she could to make things work well enough that Damian and Dario could build some kind of relationship between them.

He, meanwhile, had deliberately misled her and then kidnapped her child.

Which made what she had to do easy, she decided then and there, braced against an unaffordable sink in this outrageously luxurious resort villa on the edge of the vast, uncaring Pacific.

It felt a little bit like a death, but it wasn't. It was a declaration. He'd made it, but she could answer it—and much, much louder.

Dario wanted a war, apparently.

And this time, she'd damn well give it to him.

It should probably not have come as a surprise to Dario that the child—*his* child, if any of what Anais had said to him in Hawaii could be believed—was an utter terror.

There was no other word for it.

On the fourth day of his surprise fatherhood, Dario stood in the foyer of his sprawling Upper West Side penthouse apartment with its three stories of sweeping views over Central Park, and watched the little demon who supposedly bore his DNA run in screaming circles for no apparent reason, putting priceless artifacts at risk with each lap around the expansive living room.

"I don't understand why you haven't handled this," Dario said coldly to the nanny who'd come with the highest of references from the most prestigious Manhattan agency, which normally boasted a waiting list years long. "Why you haven't done whatever it is I'm paying you to do to stop this kind of insanity at six-thirty in the morning."

"I'm a nanny, Mr. Di Sione," the woman replied crisply, with the hint of an English accent Dario was ninety percent convinced she faked for effect and her arms crossed over her ample bosom. "Not Albus Dumbledore."

The tiny creature, who was, as far as Dario had been able to tell, made entirely of howls and fists and a boundless, terrifying energy, stopped of his own accord then and shouted something incomprehensible at Dario.

"Can you translate that?" Dario asked the nanny in the same cold tone. "Because if you can't, I might as well fire you and locate a zoologist."

"I'll handle him," the woman said with a sniff.

"See that you do," Dario gritted out, and then he stalked for the door.

None of this was going according to plan.

You do understand that he's an entire little person all his own, don't you? Anais had asked him back in Hawaii. *If you have some fantasy in your head about an angelic creature who will gaze at you and call you Daddy and serve as some kind of appendage to your whims, that's probably not Damian.*

It was definitely not Damian.

"Go to hell," he gritted out as he stabbed at the button of his private elevator, and he hoped Anais heard that, wherever she was. Lying in a heap on some Hawaiian floor, he hoped—and he told himself that pang he felt at the thought was the thrill of his victory over the woman who had wronged him, not something a whole lot more like shame.

He felt slightly more in control when he got to the ground floor of his building and pushed his way out into the sweltering heat of another Manhattan late-summer morning. He waved off his driver and walked instead, thinking the exercise would clear his head. Something had to, or he thought he might implode.

The child—*his son*—was only part of it. The truth was, he'd expected Anais to appear on his doorstep within twelve hours or so of that morning-after phone call, and she hadn't. He didn't know what to make of that. Or, to be precise, one irrepressible part of his body knew exactly what to make of it now it had tasted her again—it counted this as an unacceptable loss and wanted her even more—while the rest of him was as close to confused as he'd been in years.

Not *confused*, exactly, he corrected himself as he strode down Central Park West toward the ICE headquarters farther south. He was only dimly aware that the other pedestrians cleared the way before him, which probably meant he was scowling ferociously. But he refused to call it *confusion*, this heavy, spiked thing in him. It was anger. It was self-righteous indignation, and he'd earned it, by God. It had nothing at all to do with the bright images of their night together that coursed through his head and made him worry he might embarrass himself in the middle of corporate meetings. Nothing to do with that at all.

It came down to one simple point, he told himself as he walked toward his office. If it was all right for Anais to raise their child without him, well, then, that must mean it was all right for him to do the same thing.

Even if the child in question appeared to be the spawn of the devil on an extended sugar high.

His phone kept buzzing in his pocket but he ignored it. It was either a member of his family or of his staff. The earrings Giovanni had demanded he find were the lesser of the two priceless items Dario had brought back from Hawaii, and he kept forgetting he needed to get them out to the Hamptons and into his grandfather's hands. He made a mental note—because delivering the earrings would stop the calls at least.

And the office could damn well wait until he got in. He'd only fire everyone who crossed his line of sight in his current mood, and more than that, he'd probably enjoy it a lot more than was good for anyone involved. He kept walking. Slowly, surely, the more blocks he covered the more New York worked its usual urban magic on him, the rhythm of the city getting into his blood the way it always did. One block, then another, and he felt the cloud of it all shift, then begin to lift. He was almost feeling back to his normal self when he stopped at a newsstand outside his office building for the paper.

For the first time since he'd turned his back on a stunning tropical view to find his past standing in front of him in a long black dress, Dario felt pretty good.

Until, that was, he saw his own name splashed across the tabloids. Bold and unmistakable.

For a moment he didn't move. He couldn't, no matter how the man behind the counter glared at him and the people behind him muttered. He stared at the obnoxious headlines in sheer disbelief, as if that might make sense of them.

It didn't.

Di Sione in Bitter Custody Battle with Secret Wife—"He Wanted Nothing to Do with Me or My Baby Until Now!"

"He Left Me Years Ago to Make His Fortune, but Now He's Stolen My Baby," Cries Abandoned Anais!

Is ICE'S Front Man Cold Enough to Kidnap His Own Child?

And there was Anais's face, treacherous and tearstained, as if she'd camped out in front of the paparazzi giving interviews. It occurred to him that she must have done exactly that. She was front and center on the three largest tabloid papers, her supposedly heartbroken photos side by side with the harshest-looking pictures Dario had ever seen of himself. He couldn't imagine where they'd even found such photographs. He looked like a serial killer.

His stockholders were unlikely to find any of this particularly delightful.

Gritting his teeth, Dario pulled out his still-buzzing phone. Marnie, repeatedly, with a series of 911/SOS texts besides. His lawyers, every fifteen minutes to the second. Numbers he assumed were the usual carrion crows of the so-called press, looking for his response or his reaction, as ever. Some of his usually hands-off siblings, no doubt almost as astonished to discover they had a previously unknown nephew as he'd been to find out he had a son. And his grandfather, who surely deserved better at his advanced age than to see another one of his descendants splashed all over the papers in yet another scandal.

He didn't return any of the calls.

He stalked into the cavernous entry hall of his building and stood stonily in the elevator as everyone else in it pretended not to stare at him, and he wasn't at all surprised to find Marnie waiting for him when he arrived at his floor.

"I'm so sorry," she began the moment he stepped out of the elevator car, which was never good. "I assume you know about the tabloid situation?" He only glared at her. "Of course you do."

"I'll want a copy of each paper that ran this story and the direct number of its managing editor within the hour," he bit out.

"Of course, but—"

Dario didn't wait to hear *but what*. He started moving toward his office in the far corner of the otherwise open, wood-and-steel space, Marnie scurrying along beside him.

"Get Legal on it. I'm not afraid to take every last one of them to court for publishing this crap."

"Yes," Marnie said, "I will, but really—"

He raked a hand through his hair and unclenched his teeth. Or tried, anyway. "Do we know if the stock has taken a hit? Has it gone that far?"

"Mr. Di Sione, I'm sorry, but she's here." Marnie took a deep breath when he scowled at her, but then pushed on, confirming that this unpleasant day really had gone from frying pan to fire, just like that. "Your—Mrs.—*Anais* is here. In the conference room, waiting for you. Right now."

CHAPTER SEVEN

DARIO STOPPED WALKING. Abruptly.

He was aware of too many eyes on him, from people who should have been concentrating on their work instead of on this explosion of his personal life into the public domain. God, but he hated this. He'd hated it when he'd been a kid and his parents' tempestuous lives and tragic deaths had brought the Di Sione family entirely too much unwanted attention. It was worse now.

And even so, he was aware that what leaped in him at the sound of her name was not quite temper or fury or any of the things it should have been. It was that traitor inside his chest, and worse, entirely too much of that same old hunger he'd dared to imagine he'd slaked the other night.

What a laugh. There was no slaking his desire for Anais. There was only indulging it or recovering from that indulgence, and nothing in between.

Dario tried to focus on his secretary. "I was unaware that I'd lifted the standing security alert on her. She should be in a jail cell, not polluting my conference room."

"Yes, well." Marnie shifted her weight from one foot to the other, but held his gaze with such directness it made her sleek, steel-gray bob shake slightly where the razor edge of it scraped her chin. "She told the security officers downstairs that if they didn't let her come up she'd hold a press conference on the front steps. I thought this was better."

Dario made a low noise that was far too close to a growl, but he knew it wasn't Marnie's fault. And there were a thousand things he could have done then. He could have turned and left the building. He could have had Anais wait for him all day while he dealt with the piles of actual work he needed to do. He could have had her thrown out, anyway, and damn her threats.

He didn't do any of those things.

And later, he couldn't remember leaving the

elevator bank at all, but there he was, pushing through the glass doors of the conference room, every atom of his being focused on the slender woman who stood at the windows with a studied insouciance that made his blood boil.

And other parts of him stand up and pay far too close attention.

"The tabloids?" he demanded as he strode inside, and he made no attempt to keep the fury from his voice. "Is there nothing you won't do? No depth too low for you to sink?"

Anais shrugged, but she didn't turn from the stretch of windows across the back of the room, with skyscrapers and the distant Manhattan streets spread out before her. As if the great, sprawling city was sunning itself at her feet, the glare of the late-summer sun almost too bright to bear.

"Apparently the tabloids are the only thing that gets your attention. And you have some nerve talking about sinking to new depths, having recently transitioned from corporate shill to kidnapper."

He ignored that, along with the uncomfortable

twinge inside of him that suggested a few headlines wasn't quite the same thing as flying off
with a child, and no matter that he was supposedly the child's father. "Lying to me in private
wasn't enough for you, so you took your lurid
fantasies to the gutter press? I'd almost admire
the escalation if it weren't so calculated."

"Says the man who seduced me for the sole
purpose of abducting my child." She sniffed,
still with her gaze fixed on the city outside the
windows, her voice irritatingly smooth and cool,
like everything else about her. "You could teach
the art of calculation to one of your computers,
couldn't you?"

"Is this a competition?" His voice was not
nearly as smooth as it should have been. Dario
found that far more irritating than was at all
wise.

"You've been calling me a liar for years when
I told you the truth. I thought I'd live down to
your expectations." She turned then, and she
looked even more perfect and untouchable than
she usually did, and God help him, but all he
could think about was that wide bed in Hawaii

and the way she'd sobbed out her pleasure in his arms. Over and over again. "Where is my son?"

"*My* son. Unless you're ready to confess, at long last, your tryst with my brother? The anxious world you invited into our personal business awaits the truth."

Her gaze cooled even further, but she didn't otherwise react. Not in any way Dario could read, and he hated that. That she could still be a mystery to him and worse—that after all this time and all she'd done he could still want to solve it. What did that say about him?

But he was terribly afraid he knew the answer to that.

"You're a sperm donor to Damian, nothing more," she said quietly. Too quietly. "Rather than sort things out the proper way, you opted to become a terrifying stranger who plucked an innocent child off a playground as part of some twisted plot to make himself feel better about an imagined slight. I think your actions speak for themselves, but let's not kid ourselves. I think we both already knew you're not a very good man."

Dario would never know how he managed to

keep his temper leashed at that. How he kept his cool on the outside while inside he burned in a white-hot fury that he told himself was entirely rage—because it had to be. Because he refused to allow it be any of those darker things he hated that he could still feel for this woman.

He viewed it as a significant victory that his voice remained relatively calm when he replied to her.

"While you are, at best, a faithless cheater who will say and do anything to avoid responsibility for her own actions. Whether that's taking a lover while married or neglecting to inform a man that he has a son in the first place. Which glass house do you think will shatter first, Anais? Yours or mine?"

She smiled. Not nicely.

"I came here as a courtesy," she told him softly. "If you want a war, Dario, I can do that. I don't really care what you do to me. But you should never have touched my child. We can handle this between us like adults or we can handle it in the papers. Your choice. I have nothing to lose either way."

"How amusing that you think so."

"Public opinion tends to back distraught mothers, not the rich, terrible men who abandoned them and their own kids. Maybe you should think about that before you threaten me."

Dario didn't know he'd moved, only that he was standing much too close to her, suddenly. He could see the color in her cheeks, the hectic fury that glittered in her eyes. He was aware of the clothes she wore—a sleek shift in a deep aubergine color with a complicated neckline and another pair of extravagant, deceptively delicate-looking shoes, all her thick black hair secured in a low ponytail at the nape of her neck—but more than that, he was aware of *her*. Every breath she took. Every minute shift of expression on her lovely face. The faint seductive scent she wore, or maybe that was just her skin—

"What the hell are you doing to me?" he growled at her.

"You stole my son, you bastard," she hissed back at him. "I haven't even started yet."

And it hit him then, that she wasn't playing a game with him now. That the brittle expression behind the fury that he hadn't been able to read at first wasn't mysterious at all. It was fear.

Of him. Of what he might do.

He thought he'd never felt so small in all his life. And he couldn't understand it. Wasn't this what he'd thought he wanted? This power over her? The upper hand at last? As much his revenge as her just desserts?

"Damian is perfectly fine," Dario heard himself say grudgingly. From that tiny place inside him that hated what he was doing—hated anything that would put that sort of look on her face, no matter his reasons. "In fact, he's more than fine. He's a holy terror."

Her shoulders relaxed fractionally. Her mouth lost some of its unnatural stiffness. That frozen thing in her dark eyes thawed—if only slightly. And Dario understood that whatever else was true or not about this situation, it was clear Anais truly loved that wild creature of a child. Had he doubted that? Or had he become so used to laying every evil he could at her door that he didn't know how to do anything else where she was concerned?

The trouble was, he didn't know how to stop.

"He's not a holy terror," Anais corrected him. "Or not entirely, anyway. He's five."

"I was under the impression the two are interchangeable."

She almost smiled. Then she reached toward him as if she meant to touch his arm, yet thought better of it at the last moment. Her hand curled into a fist as she dropped it back to her side, and there was no reason on earth he should feel that as some kind of loss. Or why his forearm should throb as if it hurt where she *hadn't* touched him.

"You made your point, Dare," she said quietly. Her gaze was steady, and she raised her chin as she spoke. "You took me on quite a ride. You seduced me and abandoned me and whisked Damian away from beneath my nose. You made me feel exactly as awful as I suspect you've wanted to do for a long, long time."

She paused, and he didn't quite understand why he should feel the trickle of something entirely too much like shame move through his gut at that when it was perfectly true. When he'd done all of those things. Deliberately, if not quite as cold-bloodedly as he'd imagined he would when he'd conceived of this plan the night she hadn't let him step through her front door in Kihei.

"Don't tell me you've come here to claim you're the victim in this," he said softly, because he didn't know what to do with *shame*. It was foreign to him. It certainly had no place here, with her, of all people. Dario had built the last six years of his life on one inescapable truth: he was the victim of terrible betrayals from the only two people in all the world he'd trusted, but their failings didn't define him. He'd risen above them. There was no place in his life for shame or anything like it. "I'll laugh in your face."

"Are we finished now? Can we end this?" She kept her dark gaze on his. "Quite apart from everything else, I can't imagine you have any idea how to raise a child."

"I wasn't aware anyone did. I thought they learned it as they went, like anything else."

He could have told her he'd hired a battalion of highly trained nannies to make sure someone in Damian's vicinity knew a little something about child care, because Anais was absolutely right. He knew nothing about children save that, when he'd been one, it had been largely unpleasant until he and Dante had gone off to boarding school, where they'd had the kind of fun that came hand in hand with daily trips to the headmaster's office. He could have told her he'd never leave something like the care of an innocent child to chance.

He didn't.

"Tell me what you want," she bit out, that cool tone of hers fraying around the edges, and that didn't please him as much as he thought it should have. "To get my attention? To get your revenge? I think you've achieved that."

"I have what I want from you," he said, and he didn't realize until he'd said it that he didn't really mean it. That he'd said it simply to be cruel. Because he could. Because he was supposed to *want* to be as cruel to her as she'd been to him, surely. He should have loved nothing more than to stand there watching her press her lips together, hard, as if she was forcing back a sob, and to see how she had to fight to keep from showing him any of that.

Because there was a part of him, mean and spiked and still raw, that wanted to strike out at her however he could.

And he knew exactly what that black sludge of a feeling was as it moved through him then, rolling over him and sticking to him like a stain. He hated himself. He hated this. He hated hurting her for the sake of hurting her…

When had he become this person? This angry, bitter, horrid man who did these things with such appalling nonchalance?

But he knew. Of course he knew.

And that same old scene unfolded before him the way it always did, with the sickening inevitability of a nightmare. As if he was reliving it instead of simply remembering it. He'd gone out early that Saturday to a meeting with the people at ICE that Dante had refused to attend, in what Dario had thought was his continuing refusal to do his part in their business, and he'd been happy to be headed home after it. Anais had been the only person he could talk to back then, the only person who had understood how torn he'd felt between what he'd believed was the right thing to do for his company and the loyalty he'd felt to his brother. The fact he'd confided in her and had often taken her advice instead of Dante's was, Dario had been aware, something that had driven his brother—no fan of Anais's from the start—absolutely insane.

He could *see* the heedless, carefree way he'd walked into the apartment, throwing his keys on the same table he always did, then heading toward the bedroom to find the lovely wife he'd long since convinced himself was his perfect partner—if nothing more. Never anything more emotionally charged than that.

Because their marriage had been so analytical, so cool and careful, in the light of day. They spoke of their union as if it was a practical business arrangement they'd undertaken for the sake of their common goals with no emotional component whatsoever—and then they tore each other to shuddering pieces in bed every chance they got, again and again and again.

And she was the first person he wanted to

find when he had news to share, good or bad.
He couldn't even remember how she'd replaced
Dante in that role, only that she had. It was as
much because he and Dante had stopped thinking and acting as a single unit in those days—
the erosion of trust between them, he thought
now, that had followed that incident with the
girlfriend they hadn't known they'd had in common when they'd been eighteen—as it was because of anything Anais had done herself.

Would he have understood what all of that
meant in his own time, if she hadn't played
him the way she had? He'd already thought it
was astonishing how the two of them, raised in
such different yet similarly unpleasant circumstances by hideously selfish parents, had stumbled upon each other the way they had. Would
he have eventually comprehended what should
have been obvious to him from the start—that
their marriage had never been cold in any way
at all, and they'd only been pretending otherwise? He'd never know.

Dario could still remember the flush on her
cheeks, the wild look in her eyes, when he'd

found her standing there in the little hall outside their bedroom with one hand braced against the wall—as if she'd run to stand there, to face him. That was what he'd thought in that last moment before his whole life had imploded.

She'd stared at him, her face pale and her eyes blazing, neither of which had made sense to him. Had he moved closer to her then? He could never remember. Because that was when Dante had stepped out of the bedroom behind her, one of Dario's shirts wide open on his chest and a look Dario couldn't read at all on his face.

And Dario couldn't remember the last time he'd slept. He'd been eating and breathing the company then, juggling meetings all day and preparing for them all night. He'd barely seen his wife at all. He'd certainly not seen enough of Dante while he'd been shoving his whole face to the grindstone night after night. He'd already been feeling shut out of his own life, a stranger in the two most important relationships in his life. It had been a dark time for him already, and he'd even been *worried* about how much the only two people in the world he really cared about seemed to hate each other...

But they didn't hate each other, he'd understood then with sickening clarity. Like a kick to the gut. Clearly, that had never been what was happening between the two of them.

And that was when he'd understood exactly what Anais was to him, what she'd meant to him that whole time. Why he'd moved so quickly with this woman from the start. Why it had seemed something like *destined*, though he'd never have used that word.

Right then and there, in the hallway with his half-dressed twin, he'd understood his own foolish heart much too late.

Here, six years later in a completely different part of the city and the two of them much different people than they'd been back then, he jolted out of his ugly memories to find Anais still standing before him. Still watching him with that same arrested and fearful look on her face.

He still didn't know what it meant, what any of this meant—only that he was clearly hurting her. Whatever she'd done six years ago, whatever karmic reward he believed she deserved, *he* was the one doing the hurting now.

And he couldn't lie to himself any longer and tell himself he didn't care about that. But he also couldn't seem to stop himself.

"The only thing you could possibly do for me requires time travel," he told her, and he didn't know where that came from or why he sounded like that, gritty and nothing like calm or cool. But maybe he'd never been fooling anyone with that, anyway. "And for you to be a completely different person than who you turned out to be."

He realized he was moving as if to touch her again and he jerked himself back. That way led nowhere good, especially in a conference room surrounded by glass walls that his entire company could see through right now.

"Answer me one question," she said, her voice low and strained, though all he could see on her face was the stubborn jut of her jaw and that same glitter in her eyes. "You've made a lot of decisions based on my betrayal. The way you left then. The things you've said. The way you made sure I could never contact you and the way you ended your relationship with your brother. What if you're wrong?"

He laughed at that. "About you?"

"About all of it. About me. About your brother. About what you saw that day. Think about all the things you've done, Dare. Up to and including the kidnap of your own child, transporting him across state lines *and an ocean*, for no other purpose than to get back at me."

Her hands had curled into tight fists by the time she finished speaking, and she was trembling slightly, very slightly, as if the force of her words was tearing her open where she stood.

And Dario hated this. He hated all of this. He was afraid that what he hated most was that there was no way back. There was no pretending she hadn't cheated on him, or ignoring who she'd cheated with, and there was no making believe there wasn't a five-year-old boy in the mix now. There was no road back to what he wanted—what he still wanted, damn her, despite everything—and no way to admit he wanted it.

She was as lost to him as if he'd never met her. More, perhaps.

And what roared in him then was like a hurricane, mighty and vicious.

"That would make me a monster," he told her softly, hardly able to hear his own voice above the din inside him. "Is that what you want to hear? A petty, vicious man, much like the father you claimed to loathe before you treated your own marriage the same way he treated his. But you see, I don't spend any time worrying about such things."

"Because you're so certain you're right?" Her voice cut through the noise inside of him, that endless howl of loss. "There can be no doubt once you've made up your mind? How delightful it must be, to be so perfect and correct at all times. You must find all the rest of us mere mortals a great trial—"

"I told you before it wasn't the first time," Dario bit out, cutting her off. "Did you think you were special, Anais? Did he tell you that you were? Guess what? He lied. You weren't the first woman he sampled without my knowledge while she was meant to be mine."

He could feel the mirthless smile on his own mouth then. He could feel that hard look in his eyes, because it was ripping him apart, too. He could see the way she flinched at the sight. And he didn't tell her the rest of it—that Dante hadn't known that Lucy was playing them against each other. That they'd both gotten rid of her and supposedly moved on. That he'd had that festering distrust of his brother ever since.

Dario told himself none of that mattered. "But you were the last."

It was a war, Anais told herself, and that meant she used what weapons were available to her.

No matter how much she disliked them.

"Are you sure you want to attack a Di Sione in this way?" her aunt had asked on the drive to the Maui airport, in crisp, rapid French. The sugarcane fields had rustled on the side of the road as if they agreed, right down to their roots in the red Hawaiian dirt. "Particularly the one currently held to be the darling of the tech world, feted in every corner of the world's media? You were adamant that Damian be spared this circus six years ago."

"Six years ago Damian was theoretical," Anais had replied in the same language, the Parisian French of her childhood. The language her father had used to savage her mother, and the language both her parents had used to make certain she knew how she'd ruined both their lives and yet turned out so worthless. She kept her eyes on the fields, the windmills climbing up the rich brown mountain in the distance, and she knew her heart was already flying thirty thousand feet above her in Dario's plane and headed east. "Now he's a little boy who was abducted off a playground. If the circus is what gets him back, I'll hire all the clowns myself."

She'd meant it.

After Dario left her there in his office's conference space—the room still echoing his harsh words and what was, she supposed, the explanation for why it had never crossed his mind to believe her—she'd gotten to work.

She'd set up interviews. She'd answered all of

her texts and voice mails from all of the gutter-snipe reporters dying to talk to her so they could twist her words into unrecognizable shapes. She settled herself in the center of the long, polished table in Dario's conference room and she told her story again and again, to whoever would listen, while his employees walked by and pretended not to stare.

A few hours later, she'd spread the story of *Secretly Evil Rich Man Drunk with His Own Power* as far and as wide as she possibly could in one day. She smiled sweetly at Dario when he appeared in the doorway again.

If anything, his face looked harder and bleaker than it had before, and her tragedy was that her own heart seemed to hitch a bit at that. It didn't care that he'd done all of this to himself. It only cared that he was in pain.

She couldn't even hate herself for that. He was the first person she'd ever loved like this, heedlessly and recklessly and irrevocably. Until she'd had Damian, he was the only one. Apparently, that hadn't gone anywhere. On some level, she'd always understood it never would.

"Are you finished with whatever performance this was?" he asked in that deceptively quiet voice of his that she recognized now. It meant his temper was right there beneath it, pressing at him to escape and strike. She swore she could see it in the blue glitter of his eyes. "Some of us actually work for a living rather than spin fantasies for the paparazzi. We need access to this room."

"I was done actually." She rose to her feet and tucked her bag beneath her arm. "Did you come here to take me to Damian?"

Dario let out a short laugh. "No."

"How long do you plan to keep this up?"

His gaze was hard then. "I'm thinking at least five years. Just to be fair. I'll contact you when he turns ten."

She wanted to lunge at him for even suggesting something so hideous, but she held herself back. Barely.

"He's a little boy, Dario. He has no idea what game you're playing. He doesn't deserve this."

"He's a Di Sione," Dario countered. "He'll be fine."

She let out a low, insulting sort of laugh. "Like you are, you mean?"

He didn't like that. His eyes flashed.

"If you don't leave this office right now, Anais, I'll have you thrown out on the street," he promised her softly. Very softly. "I don't care what tabloid you hire to plaster it on their front page."

She didn't believe him. But she didn't push it. She only inclined her head and brushed past him on her way out the door.

"Remember that you said that," she advised him. Because this was war, no matter what she felt inside. No matter how much she wished it could be otherwise. He'd made it a war. He'd even taken a hostage—the only person in the world she loved unconditionally. What other choice did she have? "You might come to wish you hadn't."

CHAPTER EIGHT

DARIO WISHED A lot of things over the next few days.

That he'd thought this plan of his through, for one. That he'd paid attention to Anais when she'd warned him about the likely behavior of a small boy so far out of his element and separated from the only parent he knew for the first time in his young life.

That he hadn't imagined in all his hubris that he could simply plop a furious five-year-old into his life without any ripple effects. It wasn't as if the fact they shared genetic material could possibly matter to a small child—hell, it hadn't mattered to his identical twin brother after an entire lifetime spent in each other's pockets. He wished he'd thought a bit more before acting.

Of course, that was nothing new. It was eerily similar to how he'd felt when he'd arrived at

ICE—having left his wife and his brother and his former company behind him in a bright blaze of a burned bridge—only to discover that the owner was precisely as shady as Dante had worried he was. That all of the company's business practices were dubious and immoral, exactly as Dante had warned.

He rather doubted that a five-year-old child would appreciate the way he'd handled the ICE situation—with a systemic reworking of the company from the ground up over the course of years, which had included sidelining the owner and making him a silent partner before eventually ousting him altogether.

Dario had only spent a handful of days with Damian, but he knew full well that this child— he found it much too easy to assume the boy really was his son, and that should have worried him more than it did—was never going to be a silent anything.

"Enough," he said one morning, interrupting another tantrum. The nanny wrung her hands in the background but it had been Damian who'd picked up a two hundred and twenty thousand dollar bronze statue from the coffee table and thrown it. At Dario's head.

The fact he'd missed—by a mile—didn't change Damian's intent.

Nor did it change the fact that Dario now had a very heavy bronze stuck like a fork into his hardwood living room floor.

"I want my mom," the little boy said, his face— a perfect replica of every photograph Dario had ever seen of himself and his own memories of his brother, save those eyes that could only be Anais's—very solemn then, with his lower lip on the verge of trembling. "You said she'd come but she hasn't come."

"She'll be here soon."

And Dario wondered when he'd become such a liar. When he'd started tossing them out so easily, so readily. It made him wonder what lies he was telling himself.

"I don't like it here," Damian informed him. But it sounded like more of an observation than a complaint. "I want to go home."

"What if I told you this was your new home?" Dario asked.

Most of the residents of New York City would fling themselves prostrate on the hot asphalt street outside to get the opportunity to so much as glance inside this particular building, so famous was it after the number of colorful, wealthy characters who had graced its Art Deco halls at one point or another. And most of the world would kill for a chance to spend even five minutes in Dario Di Sione's highly coveted penthouse, and only partly because of the view.

This five-year-old who was very probably his own flesh and blood looked around as if he was deeply unimpressed, then screwed up his nose and shrugged.

"It's okay." He considered. "It would be better if my mom was here, though."

Dario met the nanny's gaze from across the room and dismissed her with a jerk of his chin, then returned his attention to Damian.

"I have something to tell you," he said. He felt like an idiot. He felt like a movie villain, ponderous and laughable, except he had no mask to hide behind while he did this. "I'm your father."

He didn't know what he expected. Something

out of a movie, perhaps. Something cinematic, dramatic. The child had flung an expensive bit of table art across the room because he'd wanted a different cereal for his breakfast—surely the news that he had a father at all should make him do…something.

Instead, Damian looked as nonchalant as if Dario had shared with him the news that it was sunny outside today, something they could both see quite easily through the sweeping windows that let in the morning light.

"I know," he said after a moment, as if the topic was boring. Stupid, even. "My mom told me. She lets me keep your picture by my bed."

"You know?" He was so dumbfounded he couldn't quite process the rest of what Damian had told him.

"She said you're very important and busy— that's why you never come to our house." Clearly tired of standing still, Damian started to fidget, working his left arm up over his head for no reason that Dario could discern. He held it there, then began to hop on his right leg. Up, down. Over and over again. "Is she coming soon?"

"Soon," Dario said absently. He couldn't quite get himself to look too closely at what the little boy had said, much less what it could mean. "You've known I was your father this whole time? Even at your school?"

"Of course." Damian stopped hopping and looked at Dario as if he was very dim. "I'm not supposed to go anywhere with strangers."

And then he started using the nearest sofa as a trampoline while shouting out the words to a song he claimed had only dog words, while Dario sat there with an unfamiliar tight feeling in his chest. He didn't know how to process this revelation.

Anais had kept a picture of him by Damian's bed? She hadn't kept the child's paternity a secret at all?

What if you're wrong? she'd asked him.

The truth was, Dario had never considered the possibility. Anais had denied it outright, but she would, wouldn't she? It had been Dante who had made him so utterly certain. Because Dante hadn't denied it. Dante had stared back at him and said nothing, not one word, his silence far more damning than anything he could have said.

And that had been a very dark time for Dario even before he'd walked into his apartment that day, but what possible reason could his own brother—his identical twin—have for lying about something like sleeping with Dario's wife?

Still, none of that explained why Anais kept his picture next to their son's bed. It was something he knew he wouldn't have done, had their situation been reversed. He would have pretended she'd never existed.

He'd told her it would make him a monster if he was the man she suggested he was. If Dante had lied, if Dario had gotten the wrong idea, if more than half a decade had ticked by like this, rolling on from that single day in his old apartment...

But he knew that was impossible. Dante had been many things back then, but he'd never been a liar—and he'd certainly never looked Dario straight in the eye and lied to him, not once in all their lives. Not even by omission.

Dario knew it was impossible.

Yet somehow, he still felt like a monster.

"What the hell are you doing?" he asked himself, almost under his breath. Because he didn't understand how Anais could be the awkward virgin he'd run after on the Columbia campus and also the woman who'd slept with his twin brother. He'd never understood that progression—and he'd never wanted to hang around and ask for explanations, either. Over time he'd thought he'd figured it out. She'd been so starved for attention, for affection, after the childhood she'd had—no wonder one man hadn't been enough for her. That was what he'd told himself. That was what he'd believed.

But a picture of him next to a child's bed didn't fit in with the character he'd imagined. With who he'd told himself she'd become by having sex with Dante for God only knew how long before he'd discovered them.

He didn't know what to make of it, and he hated that. Anais belonged in the box she'd built with her own deceitful behavior. This past week had been bad enough. Running into her so unexpectedly in that remote house on Maui, then discovering she had a child she claimed was his—it all required a somewhat larger, more unwieldy box than he'd prefer.

Still, this was worse. This struck him as an act of charity and he couldn't understand how such a thing fit with the woman who'd callously pitted one twin against the other. Who might have been doing so all throughout Dario's relationship, for all he knew.

He raked a hand through his hair and picked up his cell phone, aware that calling her was the exact opposite of how he'd normally handle something like this. Why did this woman tie him in knots when she wasn't even in the same room?

But that was when the housekeeper bustled in, placing a stack of new tabloids in front of him and taking Damian by the hand to lead him out. And instead of calling Anais to thank her for a kindness he didn't understand in the first place, he sat where he was and read capital letter denunciations of his character in as overdramatic language as it was possible to find.

The ICE Man Cometh—and He Took My Baby!

And that was when another thought occurred to him, much darker than the previous ones.

He only knew that Anais had placed a photograph next to Damian's bed. Damian hadn't specified what was in that photograph. Which meant Dario had no way of knowing which Di Sione twin was in that photograph, did he?

It was late into the night on that same day when the nanny pushed open the door to Dario's home office suite, startling him where he sat on the leather couch with his laptop and a tumbler of whiskey.

He hit a key to pause the video he was watching—of Anais on some appalling talk show, playing the part of wounded, helpless ingenue swept into all this darkness by a corporate wolf like Dario. He had to admit she was good at it.

She'd almost had him convinced he was an evil, heartless bastard and he knew better.

"I was so sheltered," she'd said, her voice choked up. *"No, he never divorced me. He simply reappeared long after I'd given up hope. I thought...I hoped... It sounds so naive to say it out loud, doesn't it? But it was all a trick. A game. He just wanted our son."*

Dario had listened to that part at least fifteen times. If he didn't know better, if he hadn't *lived* the truth of things with Anais, he'd have sworn she hadn't been acting. And even though *he knew* that was impossible, he'd found himself reacting as if she really wasn't putting on a show. As if he really had swooped down upon her like some angel of death, six years ago and now, and ruined her life each time.

She has some kind of magic power, Dante had shouted at him a long time ago, when Dario had first wanted to accept the offer from ICE and Dante had been so adamantly opposed to the very idea. He'd made the mistake of mentioning that Anais thought it made good business sense. *To make you think up is down and black is white. What's next, brother? Will she make me your enemy?*

But no. The two of them had done that together, in Dario's own bedroom.

He had to force himself back into the present, where the nanny was looking at him in concern and he had no idea how long it had taken him to focus on her.

"What is it?" he asked, aware he even sounded off. Wrong. Very much like a man who didn't know if he was crazy or sane any longer, and worse, was almost entirely certain he didn't much care either way.

"It's Damian," the nanny said in a hushed, hurried, almost apologetic voice that wiped all that history straight out of his mind. "I'm afraid he's sick."

"What do you mean?" Dario frowned at the woman. "He was turning cartwheels on the roof deck after dinner."

But he was already up and moving, following the nanny down the guest hall toward the room he'd set up for Damian. He walked inside and found the boy curled up on the bed, shivering and crying and obviously not all right at all.

He was much too hot to the touch, and Dario felt as helpless as he ever had in his life. He sat down on the bed and put his hand on Damian's small back, as if that might give the boy some comfort. He had a dim memory of his grandfather doing the same for him during some long-ago ailment.

"I want my mom," Damian cried.

And Dario had never felt worse than he did then. Had he really been using this *five-year-old* as some kind of pawn? To get his revenge on the child's mother? What was the matter with him? He'd thrown it in Anais's face that she was as bad as the father who'd never wanted to marry her mother and had cheated all throughout their marriage. But meanwhile, he was as bad as his own father, the most selfish creature who'd ever walked the face of the planet. He was worse. At least his father hadn't cared in the slightest about any of his kids—it would never have occurred to him to use them for anything.

He pulled his phone out of his pocket and dialed her number, not sure he'd be able to speak past the constriction of pure self-loathing blocking his throat when she answered at once.

"Dario?"

"You'd better come," he told her with no preamble. He didn't bother to keep his voice even or calm. What could that matter? "Damian is sick."

He didn't know how long it took her. It could have been a handful of minutes. It could have been hours. Time lost meaning to him as he sat there in the dimly lit room with a sick boy in his lap, trying to make soothing noises. He got Damian to stop crying, which made an exultant sort of triumph race through him—far brighter and deeper than anything he'd felt during ICE's last big product launch, which he'd previously imagined was the pinnacle of his life thus far.

Dario didn't know how to process that. He didn't know what it meant, only that somehow this small human who smelled of sweat and something sticky had managed to worm his way into places inside of Dario that he hadn't known were there. And he didn't think Damian even *liked* him. For that matter, he wasn't entirely convinced he wasn't holding his own nephew, not his son.

That didn't appear to have a single thing to do with it.

And then he looked up and Anais was there.

She charged through the door, her eyes snapping to Damian and staying there. She moved so fast her hair flowed behind her like a cloak and she came straight to him, up on her knees on the bed beside Dario to get her hands on the child's hot cheeks.

"Mommy," the little boy whimpered. He didn't seem surprised to see her, and Dario wondered what that was like. To have no doubt that the adults would turn up when they were needed. To expect it. "I'm sick."

"I know, baby," she murmured. Her hands moved all over him as she eased him from Dario's hold. She checked his forehead, his cheeks, and then she clucked her tongue and wrapped her arms around him to rock him. "You have a little fever, that's all. Do you have a headache?"

He moaned something unintelligible with his mouth against her shoulder and she nodded as if he'd made perfect sense. "That's not surprising. Let's cool you down a little bit and see if you can sleep."

She asked the nanny to get her a wet washcloth and while she waited she stripped Damian out of his sweat-soaked pajamas and then got him into a clean pair. Then she laid him down on the bed with the cool cloth on his head, her movements practiced and easy, reminding Dario without a single word what she'd been doing these last five years. She even curled up beside the little boy so he could hold on to her, and then she sang to him.

It was the most hauntingly beautiful thing Dario had ever heard. It broke the heart he'd thought she'd turned to stone and ash years before. Over and over again.

He sat there on the foot of the bed as this mother sang her little boy to sleep, and it took him long, shuddering moments to understand that whatever the truth was, he *wanted* this to be real. To be his in all its uncertainty and noise, silliness and sweetness. He wanted her to have come back to him with this funny little boy who was a perfect blend of both of them. He'd never wanted a family—he barely tolerated his own—but here, now, he wanted *this* family more than he wanted his next breath.

He wanted it almost more than he could bear.

And he could have left when Damian drifted off to sleep, but he didn't. Anais stopped singing eventually, but she didn't move, still curled up next to the boy like some kind of fierce lioness who would shred anyone who ventured near. He had absolutely no doubt that she would. And that he'd help.

"'The ICE Man Cometh'?" Dario asked into the quiet.

"If you ever try to take my child away from me again," she replied in a very soft voice that did nothing to conceal the steel in it, "I'll gut you with something a whole lot sharper than a tabloid newspaper."

He believed it.

They sat like that for a long time, with only Damian's half-snores filling the space between them.

"He already knew I was his father," Dario

heard himself say. He hadn't meant to speak. He'd meant to get out of here, in fact—to stand up and leave her here and return to his office, maybe to actually do some work this time. He had no idea why he hadn't done it. "He knew when I found him at his school. He said you kept a picture next to his bed."

Anais didn't say anything for a long time. Dario stopped thinking she would. It was enough, he thought, that they were both here, keeping this strangely peaceful vigil over a sick boy together. Silence was fine. It was more than fine.

It felt a lot like intimacy and, for once, he didn't balk at the notion.

"His best friend is a little girl named Olina," Anais said eventually, her voice sounding scratchy. She was propped up on an elbow next to Damian in the bed, her attention on him as he slept fitfully beside her. "Her father is a fireman on the island, which the kids agreed was very impressive and heroic. Olina told Damian that when she gets scared, her father promised her he'd always be there to fight the monsters or chase away the bad dreams. That she could just call out and he'd come. That was what fathers did, he told her. That was what they were for."

Anais shifted then, her dark gaze finding Dario's in the dim light, and he felt everything inside of him go still.

"Damian asked me how he could call out for *his* father when he didn't know where you were."

Dario was stricken, held fast in some awful grip that he thought might crush him to dust where he sat—but he couldn't bring himself to look away from Anais. Not even to blink.

"I told him that you knew where he was and that all he needed was the reminder of you to fight off the bad dreams and bad things that sometimes turn up in a little boy's closet." She didn't drop her gaze. "I said you were magic. That all fathers were, but especially you."

"Anais."

But she didn't seem to hear him.

"So together we picked out a picture of you from the photo album I have from our wedding day, and then we went to the store and found a frame he liked. He wanted double protection, just to be sure. So it's a Batman frame with you in it looking very magical and fierce and capable. It sits by his bed, and sometimes I catch him talking to it like you're real. To him, you always have been."

Dario couldn't speak. He ran his hands over his face and wasn't entirely surprised to find he was shaking.

And she wasn't finished.

"This thing you did—flying him across the world and whatever you've been doing these past few days? Playing daddy games and indulging yourself? I knew you wouldn't hurt him. I knew he'd be okay. That he'd think it was all a grand adventure with a character he already thinks he knows. You're as real to him as anything he's seen on television, that's all. *This* won't hurt him. He's a resilient kid."

And her gaze seemed to get darker then. Harder. She seemed to reach across the bed and tear him wide open when he knew she hadn't moved an inch. He could see she hadn't moved at all.

"It's when you get bored with this game. When you remember that you're *Dario Di Sione* and you have computer accessories to build and adoring customers to wow. When you throw him back where you found him and forget all the dazzling promises you made him. That's what concerns me, Dare. Because that's when you're going to break his heart."

"I'm not going to break his heart. I'm not going to break anything."

But he didn't believe that even as he said it.

"You swooped in and spirited him away. You're mysterious and fancy and you haven't disappointed him yet," she said.

And she didn't look fierce any longer; that was the part that punched at him, like a fist to the gut. She looked sad. Terribly sad.

"But you will. He'll think it's him, that there's something he could have done to make you stick around. That's what children always think." She shook her head, and looked even sadder, if that was possible. "It would have been kinder to let him keep imagining you as the perfect hero who saves him from bad dreams. Not the real, live man who hates his mother and doesn't have time for him. That's a very common, very boring story. I think he'd prefer to keep you magic. Keep you his."

"Are you talking about him, Anais?" he asked softly. "Or you?"

The way her mouth curved then made him feel scraped raw.

"I gave up on magic a long time ago," she said in the same tone he'd used. "And you were never mine."

He should never have said such a thing. He should never have opened that door, because he didn't like what was behind it. At all.

"I'm not going to do any of those things." He gritted it out, not sure why he felt so defensive. So...exposed, as if he was the one with the dirty history of letting people down instead of her. "None of that is going to happen."

And Anais laughed softly then. Still so sadly, as if it had happened already. As if she knew the bleak future before them, no matter what he said.

"Come on, Dare," she said quietly, piercing him straight through. "You can't help it. It's who you are."

CHAPTER NINE

DAMIAN WOKE UP the next morning fully restored, as if he hadn't had any kind of fever at all.

"He was sick," Dario said flatly over coffee, while Damian chased his own shadow around the expansive roof deck that surrounded the penthouse's lowest level. "I felt his forehead myself."

"Children are mysterious," Anais replied with a shrug.

And so was everything between the two of them, she couldn't help thinking. She expected him to throw her out. She'd been expecting it since she'd woken up this morning, curled up with her squirmy child in a narrow twin bed. But Dario merely sat at the outside table where his housekeeper had served breakfast as if he had nothing on his mind at all. He read the stack of tabloids that had been waiting for him, with ancient pictures of the two of them splashed all over the front pages right there in front of her, but aside from directing a particularly blue look at her now and again, he said nothing about them.

So Anais said nothing in reply, and told herself it wasn't avoidance, exactly. It was strategy. She drank his excellent coffee and she sampled his housekeeper's miraculously fluffy omelets, and she told herself it didn't make her weak or compromised that she didn't try to beat his head in with the serving utensils after what he'd done. Damian was fine, and she was with him again. That was what mattered.

She told herself that was the reason she held her tongue.

When Dario left for work later that morning he asked her where she'd been staying and she braced herself to be tossed out—but he only nodded when she told him the name of the unremarkable hotel in Midtown she'd found at the last minute, then was on his way.

And he wasn't even there an hour later when a

courier arrived at his front door with her bags. Or when the housekeeper very efficiently whisked them away and set Anais up not in a room in the guest wing near Damian, but in the room directly opposite the master suite on the top floor.

She should protest all of this, she knew. She should have taken Damian and raced off the moment Dario had left the house this morning. Or at least she should have demanded that they discuss things now that they were all together instead of hurling insults at each other in a conference room or through the papers. She told herself she'd do so the moment he returned from the office. But the nanny took Damian out to the park and left Anais to her work. She made her usual calls and caught up on all the things she'd let slide since Dario had turned up on the island. And when Dario came home in the evening to the meal the housekeeper had prepared for the three of them, it seemed much easier to simply roll with that.

And then keep rolling, one day into the next.

The less they discussed the serious issues that hung between them like so many shimmering veils—the less they talked about what was happening between them, or the dark past they'd never agree on, or what had led them to end up in this penthouse together with the child they'd made—the easier it was to keep right on rolling.

As if this was their real life. As if this was who they were, this...*family unit.*

Every night, weather depending, they would eat dinner together out on that roof deck. The three of them, together.

Like a real family, Anais thought every time, and she knew how dangerous that was. She knew that the dream she'd succumbed to that one night in Hawaii was nothing next to this one, and that single night had put only her heart at risk, not Damian's, too. But she couldn't seem to stop herself from indulging.

She thought Dario felt it, too—the insistent, beguiling tug of the sweet life that wasn't theirs.

But it could be, that seductive voice whispered inside of her, night after night. *It could be exactly like this...*

It was a treacherous landscape to navigate, and every day it got a little bit harder.

Damian loved Dario. Instantly and wholly. That much was clear, and it made Anais feel a little bit bruised inside that he'd had to do without his father all this time. It wasn't that the life she'd given him hadn't been good, it was only that *this* life—this make-believe fairy tale of a shining existence complete with a mother *and* a father all for him—was that much better.

She'd loved Dario six years ago and she despaired of the fact she loved him still, but she thought she hadn't really known what love was at all until she'd rushed through that door to find him cradling their sick son in his lap. Or when she'd watched him read Damian a bedtime story, doing all the voices. Or the many times he let Damian beat him at the video games the five-year-old adored and the grown man clearly enjoyed just as much.

Anais had always thought love was about tempestuous romances followed by years of emptiness and loss, recrimination and regret. That was what her parents had taught her, in their sad, angry marriage. It was what she'd learned in her own. She'd only started to understand

212 THE RETURN OF THE DI SIONE WIFE

the complexities of different kinds of love these last few years in Hawaii, with Damian and the steady support of her aunt and uncle.

But watching the man she'd loved since very nearly the moment she'd met him take care of the child they'd made together was like watching a new sun dawn on a brand-new world. She certainly couldn't rip Damian away from it. She hardly knew how to contain the joy of this thing she'd barely dared to dream inside herself.

She wasn't sure she managed it at all. She wasn't sure she tried very hard, come to that. And she knew, deep down, it would be one more thing she paid for in the long run.

One night they'd followed their usual pattern. They'd had a carefree family dinner, one marked by their usual easy conversation that never strayed from their preferred path of light, airy, unobjectionable topics, just like every other night since she'd come to stay here. And if there was a growing part of her that hated that—that wanted to dig down into this thing and see what was there beneath the surface, if anything— there was an even larger part of her that would have done absolutely anything to keep from rocking that boat. So she'd smiled and laughed. She'd meant it, the way she did each time, and then they'd put Damian to bed as if they'd been working together like this, like a perfect team, since the day he'd been born.

Anais couldn't control the rueful little laugh she let out at that notion, as Dario pulled the door to Damian's room shut behind him and they started back down the hall. She remembered going into labor all by herself entirely too well. It had been Team Her for a long time, no matter the show they were putting on now.

"Is something funny?" he asked.

She should have shrugged it off. Dario looked deliciously rumpled, the way he always did in the evenings. He'd shrugged out of his jacket the moment he'd stepped into the penthouse's foyer after work, leaving the cuffs of his dress shirt rolled up over those strong, muscled forearms. He'd raked his hands through his dark hair a thousand times or more over the course of their family evening, leaving it in that marvelously disheveled state, and his jaw sported its usual shadow at the end of the day.

Surely she shouldn't find all of that quite as delectable as she did. Surely she shouldn't even notice it any longer, much less after all the things he'd done to her. Anais kept waiting to grow used to Dario. To his undeniable appeal, all that tousled black hair and electric blue eyes. To find him a part of the scenery, nothing more. To stop being so…aware of him the way she always was.

It hadn't happened yet.

Maybe, she thought now, his eyes were simply too blue.

"Nothing's funny," she said. "Not really." Damian's door was closed and all three levels of the penthouse were quiet, hushed and still. And yet her heart was beating loud and hard against her chest as if it knew things she didn't. And she suspected it had more than a little to do with the way he stood there, watching her, an expression she couldn't quite read on his beautiful face. "We make a good team, it turns out. I suppose that surprises me."

She didn't say, *the way we congratulated our-*

selves for being years ago, before we'd ever been tested. She didn't ask him if he remembered how sure they'd been that their cool version of marriage, spiced up by those long, hot nights, could handle anything and everything.

It was one more thing to hang in all the shadows between them and pretend she couldn't see.

Anais thought he'd change the subject instantly, pretend he hadn't heard her, steer the conversation back to safe ground. But he only stood there, the light from farther down the hallway playing over his features, making him seem something other than hard as she looked up at him. Something other than the avenging angel he'd been playing for six long years, without ever relenting at all. Something she might have called wistful, had he been a different man.

She told herself she was imagining it.

"I'm no good on a team," Dario said after a while. Almost as if it hurt him to say it out loud. "I'm much better on my own."

"You don't seem better on your own, Dare," she said without thinking. Without paying attention to the precipice it seemed they were standing on suddenly, when she'd thought they were on solid ground. When she'd hoped they were. "You seem alone."

He moved as if he meant to reach out to her, then he slipped his hands in the pockets of his trousers instead, and she thought the sheen in his gaze then was much too close to misery. It echoed that feeling inside her own chest too well.

"I am alone." He shook his head when she started to speak, and Anais didn't know if he was trying to keep her from arguing with him or if it was himself he feared. "I prefer it that way."

"You're an island all your own?" It was an effort to make her voice dry, to try to sound more amused than shaken. "When you used to be a package deal? That seems a strange evolution."

"It suits me." His voice took on an edge then. "Surely you realized that six years ago."

"Six years ago I was so in love with you I couldn't see straight." Anais regretted it the moment she said it—particularly like that. So casually. Almost as an aside. He shifted, an arrested expression on his face, and she had no choice but to keep going. "I'm not sure I realized anything but that, to be honest."

And this time, the silence between them was anything but comforting. Anais was sure she could see the same old accusations right there between them, dancing in the light and landing hard on the floor. She waited for him to strike out, to knock her down with one of his well-placed barbs, to make her wish she'd never said anything at all. She already wished that.

She'd spent these strange days poking at this odd little peace they'd made, waiting for it to shatter around them, and now she wanted nothing more than for it to carry on forever.

But the look he gave her was shuttered, not cruel.

"It turns out that I have an affinity for solitude," he said in a low voice. "It's what I do best."

And that statement swelled inside of her, like a sob trapped in her chest. Only she didn't know what to cry for. The way their marriage had ended? The years Dario would never get back with his son? Or the way he stood before her now, so obviously lonely and broken and fierce, claiming he *liked it* that way?

Anais didn't know what she felt, what that sob was. What good her tears would do even if she dared let them fall. And she knew, somehow, that if she gave in to that great sobbing thing pressed so hard against her heart, if she let it burst open and drown them both, it would end this strange peace between them as if it had never been.

So instead she closed the distance between them, went up on her toes before she could think better of it and kissed him.

It wasn't a long kiss, or even a particularly carnal one. She pressed her lips to his and felt him jolt at that, felt the usual fire sear through her at that electric, simmering bit of contact. She put one hand to his rough jaw and she let the kiss linger, drinking him in, aware all the while of the way he stood too still, too tense.

When she stepped back, his blue gaze was nearly black with need.

"What the hell was that?" he growled.

"I don't know." She didn't put her hand to her mouth, though she wanted to, to see if she'd tattooed herself somehow. That was how full her lips felt, tingling with almost too much sensation. "You looked as if you needed it."

"I didn't." He bit that out, but she didn't believe him. And more, she didn't think he believed himself. "I don't."

And then he stalked away, leaving her to stand there with that great big sob still trapped in her chest, the brand of that damned kiss on her mouth and no idea what on earth she was doing here.

With him.

Playing games neither one of them could win.

The call came a few mornings later while Dario was out on his morning run. Only his secretary's personal cell phone was programmed to come through the Do Not Disturb setting he used while he ran his daily lap around Central Park, and she knew better than to use it without a damned good reason.

Before today, she'd used it maybe three other times that he could recall. Dario took his morning run—and his peace and quiet—very seriously.

"It's your grandfather," Marnie said when he answered. "He's taken a turn for the worse. He wants to see you."

After he ended the call and ran the last mile hard to get home faster, Dario realized he had no idea if he'd responded to that or if he'd simply hung up in a daze. Not that he should have been in any kind of a daze at all, he told himself sharply as the elevator rushed him up toward the penthouse again. Giovanni Di Sione was a very old man, even without the leukemia that had beset him this past year, adding insult to the laudable injury of having lived ninety-eight long years. The amazing thing was that the old man was alive at all, he assured himself, not that he'd finally met the thing that might have a chance at killing him.

It was funny how that didn't make him feel any better, the way he'd told himself it had before.

He strode into the penthouse, sweaty and agitated, and stopped when he heard Damian talking. Heedless and excited, the way Damian always seemed to be—because this child had no inkling of the possibility that anyone alive might not find him utterly delightful.

Dario remembered his own childhood. His parents' sick dependence on each other, the wildness and unpredictability that had haunted every moment of it before they'd died and the sadness that had wreathed it afterward. He'd had nothing to cling to in all the world but the twin brother who would grow up to betray him with his own wife.

His wife.

He found that word didn't infuriate him the way it had for years. Quite the opposite, in fact. He liked it.

He moved quietly through the entry hall and through the great living room, still following Damian's voice. He found the little boy in the kitchen, standing on a pulled-up chair so he could watch his mother make pancakes on the great stove Dario had never personally used.

"We have a housekeeper for that," he said, aware of two things even as he said it.

First, that his voice was all wrong. Ragged and

much too dark. It revealed entirely too many things better left hidden.

And second, that he'd said *we*. As if the fact he hadn't divorced her yet, or the fact they'd been living here together as if nothing that had happened between them mattered, made them some kind of unit they'd never been.

Six years ago I was so in love with you I couldn't see straight, she'd said that strange night in the hallway. Then she'd kissed him, sweet and devastating, in a way he could still feel inside of him. He'd spent the time since convincing himself it had been nothing more than Anais up to her usual tricks. He'd almost come around to believing it, too. The only trouble was, he'd seen that raw look in her eyes. He'd heard it in her voice.

And God help him, he'd felt it in her kiss.

He still did.

The truth was, Dario didn't know how to handle any of this. He understood the life he'd lived for the past six years because everything had been in neat, if painfully bleak, boxes and there was none of this blurring of long-drawn lines. In a way, the boxes were easier. There were no surprises, ever.

He didn't understand how his grandfather, who had once told Dario he intended to beat death at its own game by living forever, could possibly be dying this time—no matter how old he was, or how sick. It seemed impossible. Just as he didn't understand how the woman he'd married so quickly, met anew in Hawaii when he'd least expected it, then lived with again these past, peaceful weeks, could be the same woman who had betrayed him so thoroughly.

He wanted this, he thought then. That was the trouble. The real truth beneath all the rest of it. He wanted this woman in his house, making pancakes because she felt like it or because it made a little boy smile. And he wanted that little boy. For the first time since Anais had dropped the news of Damian's existence on him on Maui, Dario didn't care that no genetic test could prove who the real father was. That went both ways. No one could prove Damian *wasn't* his.

And if his grandfather was, in fact, dying, if this really was the end of the only family Dario knew—however inadequate it had been over the years—he knew that what he really wanted was for the old man to meet this small, wild boy with a Di Sione face and his mother's eyes. Even if it was only the once.

"What is it?" There was a frown in Anais's voice, if not on her face, as she slid the last pancake onto Damian's plate and then directed him to the kitchen island to eat. "You look as if there were ghosts out there on your run."

"No ghosts," he said, still not sounding like himself.

Or maybe it was that he'd known exactly who he was for six long years. He'd reveled in that definition and he'd convinced himself it was the truth of not only who he was, but who he could ever become.

And now he had no idea how he'd ever been happy with that.

Because he understood, standing there sweaty and thrown in the room in his home he used the least, watching a domestic scene that should have turned his stomach, that he'd never be happy like that again. That it hadn't been happiness, that in-between state he'd lived in all those years.

Everything had changed that day in Hawaii. Everything was different.

Him most of all. "Not just yet."

CHAPTER TEN

ANAIS HAD ONLY the vaguest memories of the Di Sione estate out in the Hamptons from her scant few visits way back when, but the old man who was the center of the family and the great house's patriarch had remained larger than life in her mind all this time.

Giovanni was exactly as she remembered him, if significantly more frail. He sat in an armchair in one of the drawing rooms of the grand old house, covered in a thick blanket, though the September day outside was warm. And he smiled as they walked in to greet him, that same old glint Anais remembered making his eyes seem much too bright for a man said to be on the brink of death.

"I should have told the world I was dying thirty years ago," Giovanni said, his voice more feeble than Anais remembered it, making the possibility of his death seem much more real, suddenly. "It brings you all running." His canny gaze shifted to Anais, then down to Damian in front of her. "And with such gifts."

"This is Damian," she said, smiling at the old man who she could never remember being anything but kind to her, no matter that her relationship with his grandson had been a mad little whirlwind with an unhappy ending. Then she smiled down at her son, taking her hand from his shoulder as she did. "Damian, this is your great-grandfather."

She thought her heart might burst wide open when her self-possessed little boy walked right up to the oldest man he'd likely ever seen and held out his hand, very much like the man she knew he'd one day become. And this time, there was someone to share that sort of wild maternal pride. This time, she caught Dario's eye and was sure he saw the same thing she did—maybe even felt it himself.

That unexpected moment of communion shook her, deep and hard, making her bones ache.

"It's nice to meet you, young man," Giovanni

said with an extra bit of solemnity in his voice, as if speaking to the future man instead of the current boy. But he looked at Dario when he continued, and that glint in his eye seemed more pronounced. "Very nice indeed."

"Behave," Dario told him as Anais took a seat on the couch opposite Giovanni. Her stomach flipped over and she realized it was because there was actual laughter in Dario's voice. It made him sound like a different person. It made him sound *alive*. It made him sound like that young man who'd chased her out of the Columbia University library on a gray winter's afternoon and had talked her into having coffee with him when she'd been convinced he was playing a trick on her. "Or I won't give you the earrings you sent me halfway across the planet to fetch for you."

"Ah," Giovanni said, sounding not in the least bit worried that Dario would do anything but what he'd asked. "My lovely Lost Mistresses are coming back to me at last. Tell me they still sparkle the way I remember them."

"Of course they do, old man," Dario replied,

still with all that rich amusement in his voice. It was mesmerizing. It seemed to wrap around her and pull taut, like a slipknot she feared she'd never work loose. "They're made almost entirely of diamonds. They make the night sky look dull in comparison."

The old man smiled and then coughed. And coughed. So hard his whole body shook and his hands trembled, and that was when Anais understood that this wasn't some kind of merry joke. Giovanni was truly ill. The force of his personality couldn't change that. Nothing could.

Dario's smile faltered, but he caught himself. Visibly. Anais felt a lump grow in her throat as he reached into his pocket and pulled out the same little box she'd given him in Hawaii. When Giovanni was sitting upright in his chair again and his breathing was less labored, Dario cracked it open and placed it carefully in his grandfather's parchment-pale hands.

"I wish Dante were here," Giovanni said, gazing down at the earrings, a faraway look on his face. "He always has appreciated the shiny things in life just a little bit more than you. You always did think you needed to be the serious one."

Damian chose that moment to stage-whisper his desire to go outside and play, but there was no mistaking the way Dario stiffened at the mention of his twin's name, no matter Anais's momentary distraction. Or the way that long-lost laughter disappeared from his blue gaze and the curve in his mouth flattened out into a line, as if both had been figments of her imagination.

"Why would you bring him up?" Dario asked tautly. "Is he here?"

His grandfather looked old then. Every inch of his ninety-eight years.

"I believe he's out for the day," he said with obvious reluctance.

"I'm not talking about Dante," Dario told his grandfather gruffly. "Ever. And we don't need you meddling, Grandfather. He doesn't need to know I was here."

Giovanni eyed him as if he was inclined to argue, but then merely nodded his head weakly before returning his attention to the open box in his lap. He ran a finger over the bright face of one of the earrings. Then he quietly asked Dario about ICE's much-publicized launch a few weeks back.

While Anais sat frozen on the couch across from them, her heart in a thousand pieces all over the priceless carpet at her feet.

Through the windows she could see her beautiful little boy running in gleeful zigzags on the great lawn, as if the September sun shone for him alone. But here inside this room, an old man was dying after nearly a century on this earth and the man she'd loved for far longer than was wise or healthy was so closed up inside he might as well be dying, too.

Dario was never going to change. He didn't want to talk about his twin to his own grandfather—or at all—even all these years later.

He was never, ever going to believe her.

He was fine with these make-believe spaces, these in-between times, when they pretended nothing was wrong. Meanwhile, the past festered between them. Where would it come out? It was one thing for Dario to periodically vent his spleen on her. Anais could take it, no matter how unjust it was. But what happened when he said the wrong thing one day and Damian heard it?

Because that would happen. It was inevitable.

And she couldn't stand by and allow this man to break her son's heart, simply because he didn't have it in him to trust her.

It was high time she was honest with herself. Dario had never trusted her in the first place. He couldn't have, or he'd never have misinterpreted the scene he'd walked in on that terrible day. He'd never have believed the worst of her, no matter what Dante did or didn't say.

That was the truth she'd been hiding from all this time. Dario had *wanted* to believe the worst of her. He'd seized the opportunity to leave her and he'd made sure there was absolutely no way she could prevail upon him to reconsider. He'd seen an opportunity to get the hell out of their marriage and he'd taken it.

He'd wanted to leave her then; he'd done it with surgical precision, and he'd had no intention of returning to her. Ever. If she'd never had Damian, she imagined that scene on Mr. Fuginawa's lanai would have gone very differently. He'd have insulted her, she'd have returned fire and he'd have swanned back off into the ether.

You've been lying to yourself for a long, long time, she told herself now, watching Dario laugh with his grandfather in a way she hadn't seen him laugh with anyone in years. In a way she'd forgotten he'd ever laughed, even with her. *Those stories you told the tabloids might as well have been the stories you told yourself all this time. That there was some grand misunderstanding. That left to his own devices, away from his brother, none of this would have happened.*

It would have happened. He wanted it to happen. He made *it happen.*

She sat so still, while everything inside of her spun around too fast and made her worry she might simply fall over with the force of this realization.

And she couldn't push this or any other truth on him. She couldn't *make him* believe her. She couldn't prove Damian was his and she couldn't prove she'd loved him and she couldn't prove there'd never been anyone for her but him, ever.

He would have to take that leap of faith on his own; and here, now, in the lovely home where she'd been reminded of the man she'd fallen in love with in the first place, Anais understood that he was never, ever going to do that.

He was never going to trust her, or anyone, no matter what.

And that meant that despite what she felt and had always felt, despite what she still wanted, despite the things her traitorous little heart demanded even as it broke inside her chest, she had to end this.

She had to take Damian and go home.

CHAPTER ELEVEN

IT WAS LATE that night when Dario gave up on trying to sleep in the bed he now found far too empty, when he'd never shared it with another soul. He found himself out on the great balcony that surrounded the master suite and the rest of the top floor of the penthouse. The September night was a warm caress against his bare skin, just the faintest hint of the coming fall in it, and he was glad he hadn't bothered to pull on anything more than a pair of loose black trousers.

Manhattan stretched out in the dark before him, as exultant and bright as it always was, and it echoed deep within him. It played through him like a long, low note of music, altering everything it touched. Knocking apart those careful boxes of his and making him wonder how he'd ever lived in them. How he'd ever managed to survive like that, bound and minimized. For a long while he stood there, simply stood there in the night with the city beneath him, and did nothing at all but breathe.

He sensed her approach in the moment before she appeared there at the rail beside him, her long black hair tumbling over her shoulders as straight and glossy as ever and her lovely arms bare. She wore a tank top and a pair of men's boxers, the very same uniform she'd worn to sleep in for as long as he'd known her. Dario couldn't have said why the sight of it tonight swelled inside him like a song.

He only knew he wanted to sing it so loud he woke the neighborhood. The whole city and all the boroughs. The world.

He settled for turning toward her instead, reaching out to trace a faint pattern down one slim, strong arm and taking note of the goose bumps that shivered alive beneath his touch.

"Life is so short," he said, and he felt her tremble slightly at that beneath his fingers. "Too short, Anais."

She glanced at him, then away, her gaze on the

dark heart of Central Park below them. "I know. I can't imagine the world without him."

Dario hadn't been thinking of his grandfather, or not directly.

"He's wily," he said. Because Giovanni always had been. Because he couldn't conceive of anything getting the better of the old man, even leukemia. "He's beaten a thousand enemies in his day, and is never quite as fragile as he looks. I wouldn't count him out yet."

She smiled. And she didn't say what she must have been thinking then—what he knew he ought to be thinking himself. What he'd thought explicitly, in fact, even as he'd arrived in Hawaii and had found himself marooned in all that dangerously seductive tropical heat. That Giovanni was ninety-eight years old. That there was a natural order to things. That living too long must sometimes seem as much a curse as a blessing to a man who had once been so active and was now confined to a few rooms in a house.

She only smiled, this beautiful woman who was still, astonishingly, his wife.

His wife. That was the part that mattered. That was the only part that mattered.

"Anais," he began, his voice serious, because this was long overdue.

But she surprised him. She turned toward him and she shook her head, and when he didn't continue speaking she stepped closer and slid her hands up over the planes of his bare chest. Heat against heat.

And everything inside him burst into flame.

"I don't want to talk," she said, and there was something about her voice. Or maybe it was the way she looked at him, with that gleam of something he couldn't quite read in her eyes. "I want to say a thousand things to you, Dario, but I don't want to talk."

And she was so close, after everything that had happened. And he wasn't playing any games this time, the way he'd tried so hard to pretend when he was on Maui. Her hands were on his bare skin and she gleamed pale and smooth in the light from the city around them, and he was only a man.

"I think we can figure out a better way to communicate," she whispered.

And Dario didn't have it in him to refuse her.

He didn't have it in him to try.

He swept her closer and she was against him then, all those sweet, lean curves pressed tight to him as he bent down and took her mouth the way he'd wanted to for days and days. A lifetime or two, by his reckoning. Every time she laughed, or was still. Every time she frowned at him, or simply breathed the same air.

He wanted this. He wanted her. He wanted *all* of her.

The kiss was a lick of pure fire, of blinding need. And it wasn't nearly enough.

He let the wild thing inside him loose, claiming her and marking her, tasting her deep. And as he kissed her he backed her across the smooth stone deck toward the glass doors that led inside his suite, pulling his mouth from hers only to tug the tank top up and over her head.

Her laugh as she lifted her arms to help him was better than the city's bright gleam, and it moved inside him like the same restless song.

By the time they made it to the side of the wide bed he'd never imagined he'd share with anyone, they were both breathing much too heavily, their clothes strewn behind them in a trail.

"You're perfect," he told her, his voice a guttural rasp against the dark. "You're so damned perfect."

"That sounds like talking," she teased him, nipping at his chin.

And he worshipped her, this woman he'd never recovered from and never gotten past. This woman he'd never divorced, across all these years.

Some part of him must have known it was never over between them. It was never finished, no matter how it seemed. The hunger went on and on and on.

He knelt before her by the side of his bed and he relearned every inch of her gorgeous body, the way he had the night she'd trusted him with her innocence. From her marvelous collarbone to the exquisite arch of her narrow feet, he memorized her. He studied her and he adored her.

With his hands and his mouth and his gaze,

he made her his and he made her come. Once. Again.

And the third time he threw her over that edge, this time with two fingers deep in her soft heat and his mouth a small torment against one perfect breast, she cried out so hard and so long he thought she might shatter his windows.

He almost wished she had.

"Enough," she managed to say, spread out across his bed like a feast. "You'll kill me."

"You say that as if you'd mind."

Her mouth curved dangerously and she rolled over, coming up on her knees beside him. "My turn," she murmured.

And she took her time.

She tortured him, with an electric intensity that might have concerned him, had she not been making him feel quite so good. She marked him with her teeth and she indulged herself in him with her mouth, her tongue, the sensual slide of her palms against his skin. She lavished her attention on every part of him, each ridge of his abdomen, the flat disc of each nipple, the line of his neck and all along his jaw, before heading back down the length of his body.

She smiled up at him as she knelt between his legs, something particularly raw in her dark eyes. But before he could question her, she leaned forward and took him deep in her mouth.

He thought he might die. He swore he had. He forgot everything in the world but this. Her. *Anais.*

Her mouth was hot and wet, a benediction and a prayer, and he lost himself in the slide and the suck, the small humming noises she made, the way she rocked herself as she moved over him as if she was as carried away by the sensation as he was.

It was heaven. It was too good. It was so good he thought he might lose his head completely.

He pulled her off him, his jaw clenched tight as he fought to bring himself back under control. He dealt with the condom swiftly and then he was rolling them both over and bringing her beneath him to thrust himself home at last.

She cried out at his slick possession, and then, at last, he began to move.

And there was no skill in this tonight, no mastery. It was raw and intense, wild and hot. A stripped-down taking. A claiming, elemental and fierce. She wrapped herself around him and dug her nails into his skin, and he pounded into her with all the fury of this thing between them in each and every deep, perfect stroke. He lost himself in the fit of her, so gloriously right beneath him and around him, as if they'd always been meant for this.

And for a while, there was nothing *but* this.

But then Dario could take no more. He reached down between their bodies and pressed against the center of her need, making her throw back her head and cry out his name. Then she bucked against him, writhing out her pleasure, and he hurled her straight over the side of the world.

And he followed right behind her, her name on his lips all the while, as if those long six years had never happened.

Dario knew Anais wasn't in the bed when he woke up the next morning.

He knew it in the same instant he opened his

eyes and blinked in the morning sunlight, long before he turned his head to see the wide mattress as empty as it always was. As if her presence here last night, her body tucked against his as they'd finally drifted off to sleep together, had been nothing but a dream.

If it was a dream, he'd have stayed in it awhile longer. He'd have made it last, made it count.

But he knew he hadn't dreamed a single second of it.

He swung out of the bed, pulling on the nearest pair of trousers he could find and leaving them low on his hips. He pushed his way out of the master suite to find the penthouse oddly, strangely, quiet all around him. The door to Anais's bedroom was wide open, showing him it was empty, so he jogged down the wide steel stairs that brought him to the second level. It took him a moment to realize that he couldn't hear Damian. Normally there'd be the usual clamor and howl of a young boy in the house, but not today. That was why it was so quiet.

The nanny must have taken him out, he thought absently, poking his head into one of the small reception rooms on the second level, the one Anais had claimed as her office while she'd been here. It, too, was empty. Not even her laptop open on the small, elegant desk in the corner.

Dario made his way down to the kitchen and poured himself a cup of coffee, then took it into his home office. The penthouse was still oppressively silent all around him, and there was a certain agitated sort of sensation brewing beneath his ribs. He couldn't quite identify it. He rounded his desk and sat down, frowning at the large brown file folder that hadn't been there last night, he was certain.

He picked it up and glanced inside…

And then everything seemed to turn to sheets of ice. Freeze solid, then shatter.

He understood in an instant that what had been bothering him wasn't the absence of Anais's laptop in that second-level room, but of everything else. The stacks of documents, the soft-sided briefcase she'd kept at her feet, the tangle of power cords. Or the suitcase that had sat at the foot of her bed in that bedroom across from his.

He should have realized at a glance that it wasn't her laptop that was gone. She was.

Because he recognized the document in the file folder. It was the stack of divorce papers he'd left for her in his hotel room on Maui.

A dark, terrible thing was unfurling in him, deep and wide and thick, but he made himself flip through the papers to see if she'd signed it. She had. Of course she had. Her signature was just as he recalled it, somehow perfectly French and perfectly her at once, and he thought a bullet to the chest might have been easier. Better, maybe.

He heard a sound at the door and he looked up, somehow unsurprised to see her standing there, dressed head to toe in what he knew, now, were her lawyer clothes. Cool and gorgeous and sleek.

Her armor.

He didn't beat around the bush. "Why?"

Something moved over her face, too quick for him to categorize it.

"You don't trust me," she said simply. "You'll never trust me."

"This can't possibly—"

"Dario."

He stopped, though he thought it might have broken something inside him. He didn't know how there could be anything left to break.

"I can't live like that," Anais told him, that same raw thing he'd seen in her gaze last night there again, and in her voice besides. "I grew up in a house of hatred and contempt. Terrible accusations were thrown about like they were nothing. I won't raise my son that way, surrounded by suspicion and fury at every turn."

Dario was reeling. Unmoored and untethered, and he remembered this feeling all too well from six years ago. The sick thud in his stomach. The noise in his head.

The great black pit of loss that yawned open beneath him and wanted to swallow him whole.

Last time, he'd let it. He'd jumped right in. He'd stayed there for years and called it *realism*. He couldn't bear the thought of sinking into it again. He couldn't imagine there was any way out a second time.

"And last night? What the hell was that?"

"I wanted to say goodbye," she said, and her

cool tone slipped a bit. He heard the rawness. The pain. And it didn't make him feel any kind of triumph. It was no victory. It only made him hurt. "I didn't want to walk out on you."

The way he had, without a second thought or a backward glance. She didn't say that. She didn't have to say it.

Dario rose then. He didn't know what he meant to do. If anything.

"Don't do this." He wanted to sound fierce, sure. Instead, he sounded broken. Maybe, this time, he really was. Or maybe that was the point she was making—that he had been all along. "Don't. What do I have to do to keep you here? Name it."

But Anais's expression didn't change. If anything, she looked sadder and more resolute at the same time. And he had the strangest sense of foreboding as she opened her mouth.

"Talk to your brother," she said softly. "That's what you have to do for me to stay."

"No." He gritted the word out, every part of him tense and furious and still reeling closer and closer to that great black pit. "Why would you ask such a thing? Did my grandfather put you up to this?"

And he saw the way her face crumpled, just slightly, before she blinked it away. He saw the way she clenched her hands into fists at her sides. He saw that terrible sadness in her eyes.

"The fact that you don't know is why I'm leaving." She waved a hand, taking in the room, the city, maybe. Him. "This only works if we pretend the past never happened. If you make an effort to act as if it never happened."

He didn't understand this at all. "I'd think that's a good thing, considering."

"Dare." That nickname only she had ever used, but in that hard, hurt voice, and it was worse than a kick to the gut. "I won't live my life as a hostage to a history that you've been getting wrong for six years. How can we ever move forward if you can't look at the past and see the truth?"

"This has nothing to do with that."

"There is no *this* without *that*," she corrected him. "Because *that* never happened. I don't need your forgiveness and I refuse to spend my life trying to convince you to trust me when I never broke your trust in the first place. You know what my parents were like. The screaming fights, the ugly names, the endless horror of it. I won't raise Damian like that. I don't want him to think that kind of war is love."

"It's not like that. We're not like that."

"You can't even imagine calling your brother. Your twin. You can't *imagine* it."

"Dante has nothing to do with us!" he thundered at her.

"I know," she said sadly. "And he never did. But I don't think I'm the one you need to hear that from. And I can't waste my life hoping you see the light and repair what you broke so we can all move forward. I won't."

She was really going to do this. She was really going to leave him, after everything. After they'd made it through what should have been the darkest place. He could see it on her face, in the gleam of moisture in her eyes.

He could feel it in that terrible constriction in his chest.

"Anais..."

"I'm taking Damian back to Maui," she told him, straightening in the doorway, her tone measured. As if she'd been planning out what she would say and was delivering the news to him as calmly as she could. "I'm not taking him away from you and I won't keep him from you. You can see him whenever you like. I'm happy to talk about a formal custody arrangement as we work through the divorce, but informally, I'm perfectly fine with whatever works for you."

"Those are the same papers as before," he said, unable to process this. Unable to understand. "The ones that claim you were unfaithful and name Dante as your lover."

"If that's what you need me to say in open court, then I'll say it," she told him.

And Dario understood that he should have viewed that quiet statement as his most decisive victory yet. But all he could seem to feel was a crushing sense of defeat. Of incalculable loss. Of nothing but grief, rolling on in all directions, forever.

She merely shrugged, and somehow that made it worse. "This needs to end, for all our sakes. I don't care if it takes a lie to do that, as long as it's over."

"Anais. Damn it. This is…"

"Dario." Her voice was hard then. Cold. Very serious. She waited until he met her gaze, and he knew then. He was already in that dark pit. He'd never climbed out. He never would. "You have to let me go."

CHAPTER TWELVE

IT TOOK DARIO less than a day to determine that he was not going to repeat the mistakes of the past. He refused to throw himself into that darkness and hope his work might save him. Not this time.

By the end of the day she left him, taking Damian with her, Dario was fully resolved. He stood on the roof deck without her, staring off into the hectic muddle of the city he hardly saw without her in it, and knew exactly what he wanted.

And Anais had named the single obstacle standing in his way.

Of course, he told himself then, he needed to call his damned brother.

But it took him a little bit longer to actually do it. He'd been so furious at his twin for so long. It was hard for him to let go of that.

Maybe too hard, he thought a few hours later as he waited on the same roof. Maybe some breaches were supposed to be there.

He didn't have to turn around to know that Dante had arrived. That same intuition that had seemed like magic to those around the two of them, dormant for six long years, prickled alive instantly. He knew the very moment Dante stepped out onto the roof.

He didn't simply know it. He *felt* it.

He took his time turning, and his brother was there when he did. It had been six years, and yet it felt...right.

"This is anticlimactic," he said, eyeing the man standing across from him. It was still like looking into a mirror. It was still as if Dante was an extension of himself. *This is right*, he thought again. "I thought you'd at least have the good grace to be horrifically scarred or stunted in some way."

"I could fling myself off the balcony in a show of dramatic atonement," Dante replied in his usual easy manner, though Dario could see the wariness in his eyes. "Of course, that would likely kill me instantly. Much less suffering for me that way, which I'd think would defeat the purpose."

Dario had to catch himself then, because he almost laughed at that—and this was the trouble. This was his *twin*. He knew Dante better than he knew himself, in some ways, or he had. He was genetically predisposed to get along with him. These past six years had been torture—and he couldn't understand how he'd managed to convince himself otherwise. How he'd believed his own lies.

You've been lying to yourself for a long, long time, he thought then.

"You betrayed me," he said starkly, and his brother stiffened. "That was all I knew six years ago. That was all I wanted to know. You hurt me. You, of all people."

Dante only stared back at him, the way he had then, and said nothing.

"Now I want to know the details," Dario continued. He realized he'd tensed every muscle in his body and forced himself to relax. As best he could. "Anais has a child. He looks just like us."

He searched his brother's face. His own face, at a distance, as identical as it had ever been. As children and teenagers they'd played each other for days at a time to see if anyone noticed the switch. No one ever had.

Dario forced himself to ask the question. "Is he yours?"

"No."

The word was like a stone hurled from a great height, and it landed between them with the force of too much gravity. Dario was surprised the roof deck didn't buckle beneath them with the wallop of it. He was surprised he didn't.

Dante looked stricken and fierce at once. "*No. I never touched Anais, Dario. I never laid a single finger on her. I never would.*"

And Dario realized that he'd known this, on some level. He must have known this, or he wouldn't have turned and walked away. He wouldn't have cut Dante and Anais off so completely, leaving them no recourse, if he'd thought they'd really cheated on him, because why would he have cared what they said then? And he certainly wouldn't have thrown his revenge aside, ignored the way she'd deliberately aired their private business in the papers, all for the sake of a few family dinners. Not if he'd truly believed she was trying to foist off his brother's child on him.

Because there was only one way Anais could be *so sure* Damian was Dario's. Beyond a shadow of a doubt. Only one explanation.

This was what she'd meant, he understood now. This was what she couldn't live with. It wasn't only that he'd believed the worst of her. It was that he must have been *looking* for something hideous to believe about her as his way out, because look how quickly he'd taken it. Look what damage he'd done.

What he didn't know was why.

"You let me believe otherwise," he said now to the twin who was the lost part of him. How had he pretended all this time that he was whole when that was laughable at best? He didn't care that his voice was too thick. "Deliberately."

Dante moved then, closing the distance between them to stand nearer to Dario at the deck's rail. He frowned down at the traffic on Central Park West, but Dario knew he didn't see it.

He saw the past. Dario had lived in that past for too long. He wanted out.

He wanted to be free.

More than that, he wanted his family.

"I did," Dante admitted. He shook his head. "I hated that you listened to Anais more than to me. I hated that she'd come between us when she was supposed to be nothing more than a business arrangement. You'd married her to give her a green card, not to install her as our third partner."

Lies upon lies, Dario thought, and all of them his own damned fault. "I didn't marry her to give her a green card."

Dante let out a small laugh at that. "That became clear." He shifted to look at Dario. "You were at that damned meeting with ICE. I thought she'd put you up to it, so I took the opportunity to drop by and get in her face." He looked rueful. "She doesn't back down."

"Not usually," Dario agreed. "As you've likely seen in the tabloids."

"She threw a glass of water at me." Dante moved a hand in the air over his chest. "All over me. And that calmed things down. The irony is that we'd actually started talking to each other when you walked in."

"On you. Coming out of my bedroom, half-dressed."

"It didn't even occur to me that you might read it the wrong way," Dante said in a low voice, "until you did. And I realized you'd obviously never gotten over what happened in college."

"It seemed like a pattern," Dario said then. Though in truth, he thought it was the broken trust he'd never gotten over and never forgotten—and maybe that hadn't been fair. It had been Lucy who had lied, not Dante. But he hadn't wanted to consider that back then. It had all been a mess. ICE, their past, Anais… "But Anais mattered more. Much more."

"I never meant any of this to happen," Dante said fervently. "I never wanted to break up your marriage and I certainly never wanted you to cut *me* off. I assumed things would go back to normal after you'd had time to cool down. I assumed that, at the very least, you'd come after me. Yell at me. Fight with me. Hell, I thought you'd answer the damn phone, Dario."

Dario blew out a breath. "I don't know why I didn't. I don't know why I let a moment of silence ruin two relationships." He looked his brother in the eye, then reached over and clapped his hand to Dante's shoulder. "You might have done nothing to keep me from believing the worst, Dante. But I'm the one who believed it. That isn't your fault. It's mine."

The evening wore on then, but everything was different. Better.

They sat out on the roof and told each other the stories of their lives over the past six years, and while they were no longer finishing each other's sentences the way they had as children, it was remarkably easy to get back in tune. To feel connected again. Whole.

Dario hadn't realized how much he'd missed his brother, or how deeply he'd been fooling himself all this time.

"How did you end up in Hawaii, anyway?"

Dante asked. "Didn't you once claim you didn't see the purpose of beaches?"

"Maybe I've had a radical personality transplant and now enjoy nothing more than lying on a bit of sand, waiting for death or boredom to claim me," Dario said.

Dante laughed. "Have you?"

"Certainly not." Dario laughed, too, and it felt good. It felt like a revelation, like another key turned in a lock he hadn't realized was there, to sit beneath the stars and laugh with his twin again. "I was tracking down a pair of earrings for our possibly demented grandfather."

"He sent me off to find a tiara," Dante said. He raked a hand through his hair. "Maybe this has all been an elaborate ruse on the old man's part. Maybe he didn't accidentally sell off a load of trinkets at all. Maybe they were all baubles he handed out."

"What, as gifts? Who hands out priceless jewelry as gifts and calls them 'trinkets'?"

"Remember that Grandfather's from Europe. He's very old school." Dante shrugged, that utterly familiar maverick's grin tugging at his mouth. "Maybe he took a very European view of his wedding vows and kept a string of wealthy mistresses on the side."

It was hard to imagine their grandfather doing any of the things one might logically do with a mistress—especially when the image Dario had of him now was Giovanni as he'd been at the house the other day, frail and unwell. On the other hand, the old man was famously cagey. And certainly their own father's brief, chaotic life suggested that growing up in Giovanni's house had been something less than perfect.

"The man likes his secrets," he said now.

They looked at each other, and it was back. That instant, wordless communication that the twins had once been so fluent in it had taken them longer to learn actual English than any of their siblings. They hadn't needed it.

They both pulled out their smartphones and started typing various things into the search fields of their browsers.

"'Tiara and earrings,' it turns out," Dante murmured a few moments later, "leads us directly to the Duchess of Cambridge and her pageant of a wedding. Who knew she'd cornered the market on a matched set?"

"I think we can cross Kate Middleton off the list of our grandfather's potential mistresses," Dario replied. "I feel certain the British press would have picked up on it."

But he remembered the snatches of conversation he'd heard over the past few months while he'd been concentrating on the product launch. Little snippets about family matters he hadn't been particularly bothered about at the time.

One of his brothers had found a necklace for Giovanni; one of his sisters had produced a bracelet. He put all of those together, and then threw in a description of the jewels. White diamonds. Bright green emeralds.

"Look at this," he said, leaning closer so Dante could see the screen, as well.

"They were all a commissioned set," Dante said as Dario scrolled down the page, reading at the same pace. Of course. "I'm surprised they were ever broken apart."

"It says each piece is inscribed with a word."

"Kate Middleton? I knew it."

"BALDO," Dario said, his mouth twitching. He read down further. "No one has ever been able to figure out what that means."

"That's the trouble with secrets," Dante said then, sitting back in his chair. "They must seem like a good idea at the time. Then they're nothing but old words inscribed on the back of lost trinkets, and precious few people to care."

Dante had to head out not long after, but Dario knew that everything had changed between them—and for the better this time. They might not have solved every problem, but they'd started the process.

He had his brother back. He was himself again.

The future was not going to take place in a series of little boxes. Not if he could help it.

And that meant there was only one thing left he needed to do.

It was time to head back to Hawaii and claim his family.

This time, when that same hard knock sounded on her door after dark, Anais told herself it couldn't possibly be Dario. She'd been very clear with him. She and Damian had come home and settled right back into the perfectly decent life they'd been living before Dario had made his reappearance. Everything was exactly as it had been before.

Save that Damian now had a lot more to say to the photograph by his bed, and Anais found herself curled up in her own empty bed with nothing but her broken heart. Broken even harder this time, because she'd been the one to leave.

The knock came again, even louder.

Anais took her time getting to her feet, and longer still crossing to the door. And maybe some part of her had been expecting an impromptu visit one of these days, because she hadn't changed into her usual postwork clothes. Not a single one of the nights since they'd come home from New York.

Had she been hoping he'd show up? Had she imagined that if he did, she'd really feel safer in a pencil skirt and a sleeveless blouse?

She swung open the door and there he was, and her whole body hummed to life, as if she'd locked herself away in a deep freeze here in the tropics. As if Dario was all the heat in the world.

He looked gorgeous and intent, in the kind of sleek, expensive T-shirt that only very rich men thought looked casual and a pair of jeans. He looked rugged and rumpled, his dark hair shoved back from his face at an angle that suggested he'd been raking his hands through it all day. His blue eyes met hers and held.

"This time," he said in that low voice that connected to every part of her that longed for him and lit it all up like fireworks against a dark night, "you need to let me in."

Anais didn't move. She didn't step toward him and she didn't step back. And she was terribly afraid that he could hear how hard her heart was beating in her chest, that he could see how little it would take for her to simply throw herself in his arms and wave away the past...

But she refused to do that. Damian deserved better than that.

And so did she.

"I don't think that's a good idea," Anais said, and it was one of the hardest things she'd ever done in her life. She'd thought that morning in New York had been difficult. She'd had to fight to keep herself from sobbing in front of her five-year-old on that endless flight home. But this was harder.

Because he was here. He'd come after her.

She wanted that to mean a lot more than she suspected it could.

"I meant what I said in New York," she made herself tell him, because she didn't want to say anything of the kind. She wanted to stop gripping the doorjamb. She wanted to launch herself at him. But that was always the trouble, wasn't it? She wanted things she couldn't have, and Dario was at the top of that list. "This can't work."

She expected his eyes to flash dark, for him to argue. She expected threats, harsh words.

Instead, he smiled.

That beautiful smile of his. It was like a perfect sunrise. It was entirely too much like joy, and she didn't understand it at all.

"I'm not going anywhere, Anais," he told her, as if he was reciting a vow. "I'm not walking away again. I'll stay right here on the doorstep for as long as it takes."

"You're not going to stay on the doorstep. Don't be ridiculous."

That smile of his widened. "Maybe not literally."

And she told herself she had no choice. That her heart was a terrible judge of character, or none of this would have happened, would it? She made herself step back.

"Goodbye, Dare," she said.

That smile of his didn't fade. And it hurt her—physically hurt her—to close the front door. Then force herself to walk back into her house and carry on with her life somehow.

She couldn't say she did a good job. She sat there on her sofa and stared across the room at the bookcase where her single photo album of their time together was stored, and she ordered herself not to cry.

Over and over and over. Until she fell asleep slumped sideways on the couch and stayed there until morning.

It was a new day, she told herself when she

woke up, cranky and sore. Dario had been seized with something highly uncharacteristic to come all this way and make declarations, but she imagined it was like a tropical sunburn. Painful, but it would peel eventually. Then disappear.

But he came back again that night. And the night after.

And every night that week.

Always after dark, when Damian was already in bed, so there could be no chance of using their son's feelings as any kind of bargaining chip. And he always left with that same smile on his face, as if he really could do this forever.

"I think you have issues," she told him when it continued into a second week. "I never should have gone out to coffee with you in the first place all those years ago. It set a terrible precedent. You think you can wear me down with persistence and a smile."

The scary part was that they both knew he could. She expected him to laugh, but he didn't. He stared at her, the thick dark all around him and his blue gaze serious.

"I don't want to wear you down, Anais," he

told her. "You already know that I can walk away when things get tough. Now you know that I can stick around when things don't go my way."

"What if I want you to go away?" Her voice was so hoarse, so soft. She might have thought she hadn't said anything out loud, but she could see that she had in the way he went still.

"Then you have to say that," he said. "You have to tell me there's no hope and that this is never going to change. As long as there's hope, I can do this forever. Tell me that's gone and I'll never bother you again."

And she stood there for a shuddering beat of her heart. Then another. She felt the soft breeze on her face, and curled her bare toes into the cool concrete of her front step. Everything else was the blue of his eyes, the starkness of his expression. The way he held himself, as if braced for the worst.

She should open her mouth right now and tell him there was no hope. It was the kind thing to do—the safe and smart thing to do, for everyone.

"Good night, Dare" was what she said instead, stepping back inside and closing the door.

She could feel him there on the other side. She slumped against the closed door, squeezing her eyes shut, and she could *feel* him there, only that flimsy bit of wood and her own determination separating them.

Anais didn't know how long they stood there. She'd never know how long it was before she heard him turn around and go. Or how much longer she stayed where she was, before she forced her stiff, protesting muscles into a hot shower in the hopes that might stave off insomnia. It didn't help at all.

And two nights later, she let him in.

CHAPTER THIRTEEN

ANAIS DIDN'T KNOW what she expected Dario to do. But it wasn't what he did, which was walk inside as if he'd never had any doubt she'd let him in eventually and then look around, as if searching for something.

"Do you have a fireplace?" he asked.

She scowled at him. It was lowering to realize she'd expected fervent declarations, or at least a discussion of some kind, while he apparently wanted…something else entirely. Whatever that was.

"We have a little fire pit out back," she said. "Damian likes to roast marshmallows every now and again."

He strode past her and she found herself following, then watching in some mix of astonishment and bemusement as he set about building a fire in the hollowed-out center of the table that claimed pride of place on her small patio. It had been an indulgence, that odd little table with the built-in fire pit in its center, but she'd had some of her favorite evenings here with Damian. She had no idea why Dario's being here now made her feel as if she ought to apologize for that.

"Wait here," he said when he got the fire going.

And the crazy thing was, she did as he asked. She waited. She told herself she was simply standing there, waiting to see what would happen next, but it was nothing so passive. She was terrified. She was exhilarated.

Maybe she was paralyzed.

She was too many things at once and she had no idea how she could possibly survive this. Whatever *this* was. She'd lost Dario too many times already. How much of her was left? How could she afford to risk it again?

But she knew, standing there with her eyes on the flames as they leaped against the dark, that this had nothing to do with Damian. People all over the world shared the custody of their children, and the great majority of those children were just fine.

This was about her. This was about the two of them, Anais and Dario. This was about six years ago, and this was about New York, and she didn't know if she had it in her to survive *this*.

Dario came back out on the porch, holding a thick sheaf of papers in his hand. He moved around to the opposite side of the table from where Anais was standing, and he met her gaze over the dancing flames of the fire between them.

"My father was a ruined man," he said.

He tilted the sheaf of papers he held so she could see them, and Anais caught her breath. It was the divorce papers. He'd brought them here.

Dario peeled the first page off, held it aloft, then fed it to the flames. "He was addicted to everything. You know this. He and my mother were as raucous and wild as yours were furious and brooding. I don't know that they ever loved anything. Not each other, not us." He watched her as he added another page to the fire. "After they died, my grandfather took us in, but he was not precisely a warm man. As he grew older, the stories he told were affectionate, interesting and never about us. They were always of other places, lost friends, misplaced trinkets. He was always somewhere else, even when he was in the same room."

"You don't have to tell me this," she whispered, surprised to find she'd shifted to hold herself at some point, her arms wrapped around her middle. "I know your family story."

"All I had was Dante," Dario said, as if he hadn't heard her. "He was my twin, my brother, my best friend. Truly, the first person I ever loved. I would have done anything for him. I did. And there were things that came between us before you, cracks in our relationship, but no one else I loved."

That word. *Loved.* She realized he'd never told her he loved her. She'd accepted that she'd loved him back then, but she'd never have dared to say so. That wasn't their agreement. That broke all the rules. Hearing that word in his mouth now made something inside her flutter. As if, were she not very careful, it might spread out its wings and start to fly away.

"And then you," Dario said quietly, as if he

knew. "I looked up, and there you were, and nothing was ever the same after that."

Anais held herself tighter, all of her attention—all of *herself*—focused squarely on Dario, just there on the other side of the small fire, burning page after page of those awful papers as he spoke.

"I spent some time with Dante the other day," he told her.

There was no holding back those wings inside her then. They unfurled. They started to beat. And something inside her soared.

"Then you know." She felt the wetness on her face, but did nothing to stop the tears. She couldn't move. She couldn't look away from him. "You know I never betrayed you. I didn't. He didn't."

"No," Dario agreed, and there was sheer torment in his voice, his eyes. "I betrayed you. I was so ready to believe the worst. I was so lost back then, stressed out and overwhelmed, and maybe I wanted a terrible fight so I could control something, anything that was happening to me. I walked away from the only two people I've ever loved. I told myself cutting you both off was a victory, that it was an act of strength in the face of what you'd done to me. But I understand now it was the worst kind of cowardice."

"Dario…" she whispered.

"Dante and I were twin brothers, the two of us against the world. We had our own language, our own universe. I never learned how to *work* at things. I never had to learn. I was raised by a man who ignored the present all around him, the better to drift off into the past. And my parents dealt with their problems by courting oblivion by any means necessary. Up their noses, down their throats, whatever worked."

He threw another set of pages on the fire and the breeze blew the smoke in her face, sharp and rough at once. Anais didn't turn away.

"My parents were no better," she told him. "They taught me I deserved cruelty. That I was worth nothing."

"I know," Dario gritted out. "And I will never forgive myself for sending you the same message, all because I was too much of a coward to tell you the truth. I didn't marry you because it was good business. I didn't do it out of the goodness of my heart, because you needed immigration help or because I thought an in-house lawyer would be a great idea. I married you because I fell in love with you the moment I saw you, and it scared the hell out of me."

Anais couldn't see then. Tears streamed down her face, mixing with the fire and the smoke and the thick Hawaiian night. Somehow forming a kind of paste that wrapped itself around her broken heart and made it feel whole again.

Making her imagine. Making her hope.

"I knew Damian was mine the moment I saw that photograph," Dario continued, his voice rougher than before, his gestures jerkier as he kept throwing page after page into the fire. "But more than that, I knew you. I knew you'd never throw it in my face like that if there'd ever been the slightest bit of doubt. I didn't want to know these things. I pretended I didn't know them. But I did."

He held up the last page, with both of their signatures, both bold scrawls of blue. He waited while she wiped at her eyes, her face. He waited until she met his gaze again.

"Anais," he said, "I love you. I've never loved another woman and I never will. I don't want to pretend anymore."

Then he set their divorce on fire. He held the paper for another moment, then let it go.

And then there was nothing but flames, and smoke, and love.

Their twisted, stubborn, fierce love that nothing had managed to destroy. Not betrayal. Not distance. Not her own better judgment. Not his vast wealth and ability to pretend she didn't exist. Nothing.

Here they still were, all these years later. No matter who walked away, the other one always opened the door. Eventually.

"Listen to me," he said urgently.

He moved around the table then to take her shoulders in his hands, as if he thought she planned to reject him yet again. When the truth was, she didn't know what she planned to do.

Don't you? a voice inside of her asked.

"I know this is about trust," he said, his hands

so warm against her, sending heat spiraling down into her flesh. "And I know you have no reason to trust me. I can't make you trust me or promise you I won't let you down in the future. I can only tell you that I'm not the same man I was six years ago, or even a month ago. You changed me." His hands moved to her upper arms, drawing her closer to him. "If you give me the chance, I'll spend the rest of my life trying to prove myself to you. I'll do whatever it takes."

She couldn't speak. She could only gaze up at him, almost as if she didn't believe this was happening.

"I love you," he said, and then he said it again, as if to make sure there could be no mistake. "And I love Damian. I want us to have the family we deserve, and I want to give him the family you and I never had. I want the whole package, Anais, if you'll let me. If you'll try."

And life came down to leaps of faith. Running for the edge and jumping out into nothing, hoping something would come to break the fall before landing. Sometimes it did. Other times it didn't, and that was a different lesson altogether.

But no matter how many times she'd landed on her face, with Dario in particular, there was something that made Anais want to jump all over again.

Because even if she fell, the falling would be worth it.

She had to believe it.

There was a reason she hadn't moved on. There was a reason she'd built a safe little life here, where she could pretend to be getting on with things when all she'd really been doing was waiting. There was a reason she'd never made a very good glacier. She'd made sure Damian loved his father before he'd ever met him. She'd been paving the way back to Dario since she'd left New York. How had she never realized it?

"There are no guarantees," he told her, his hands tightening where he held her. "But I can promise you this. I'll always come back to you. You'll always be my home. I hope I'll never give you reason to doubt that again."

She swayed closer to him. She lifted her hands to cup his face, reveling in the scratch of his unshaven jaw against her palms. She gazed into the eyes of the only man she'd ever loved, just yards away from where the perfect little boy they'd made together slept soundly. Maybe there were more perfect things than this, than him, but not for her.

Anais had only and ever been destined to be right here.

"I love you," she whispered, and she watched that go through him like a wave. "I've always loved you." She went up on her toes and she wrapped her arms around his neck, getting her mouth so close to his she could almost taste him. "And we'll try together, Dario. Again and again and again. Until we get it right."

And then she started off their future with the perfect kiss, right there beneath the dark Hawaiian sky, with nothing left between them but love.

At last.

Love was the easy part, Dario thought a year later, as he stood outside that same villa at the luxury resort in Wailea and gazed at the beautiful woman who was not only his wife but the true light of his whole world.

Trust took time.

There were no boxes in this life they'd built together, day by day. There was a great deal more laughter. There were perfect nights and stolen moments they found when they could. They'd learned to split their time between New York and Hawaii. They'd learned to talk more and walk away less.

They taught each other how to try, every day. Sometimes they failed. More often, they got there. Wherever they were going, they got there. Together.

Today, Damian stood between them, all three of them with their bare feet in the sand of the private beach. They'd recited a few vows, though their child had declared that "weird."

"It's called renewing our vows," Dario told him.

"Do all married people do that?" Damian asked.

"Only the lucky ones," Anais told him, her dark eyes warm on Dario's.

Damian seemed to accept that, grown-up six-year-old that he was, or perhaps his focus was on other things.

"I thought you said there was going to be a present." He grinned angelically when both his parents frowned at him. "I like presents."

"Holy terror," Dario mouthed to Anais.

Her mouth twitched as she ran her hand over Damian's head.

"What have you always said you wanted more than anything in the world?" she asked him.

"A brother," Damian replied instantly, and when she smiled, he whooped. Then took off to run wild circles up and down the small beach, shouting out his excitement to the surf.

"I hope you're ready for another one," Anais murmured, wrapping her arms around Dario and tilting her head back to gaze up at him.

"I've never been more ready," he promised her gruffly. "Trust me."

And this time, when she gave birth to his son six months later, he was right there beside her. And the very first thing little Didier ever saw.

It got louder and it got messier, and the truth was, Dario loved it. He'd had no idea that he could love so much and so many. His brother was back in his life where he belonged, and better this time, since Dario appreciated what they shared—their twin bond—in a way he never had before. He'd had no idea how much he'd craved the kind of family bonds and deep intimacy he'd thought he'd wanted nothing to do with.

"I have something to tell you," Anais said a couple of years later.

They'd come to Maui for Damian's school vacation, and were sitting out on the lanai of the house where they'd met for the first time six years into their marriage, the house Dario had bought from the Fuginawa estate after the old man had passed on. The rolling hills of the Kaupo countryside gleamed beneath the stars and, far below, he still thought he could hear the sea.

"Because all good conversations start exactly like that," Dario murmured, pushing his laptop aside and closing it. Focusing on Anais. He didn't like the way she stood there, almost mimicking the same positions they'd taken all those years ago, so he hauled her into his lap and got his mouth on her neck.

The same fire roared between them. It always had. It always would.

A wave of goose bumps washed over her, and she shivered in his arms, and only the presence of his children in this house somewhere kept him from pulling up that loose dress she wore and making them both a whole lot happier, right here.

"Remember how I told you I didn't feel well?" she asked, angling her head to one side to give him better access.

"I do." He pushed the silk of her hair aside and trailed heat along the line of her neck. "Remember how I told you my theory and you assured me you couldn't possibly be pregnant?"

She didn't reply and that old fear gripped him—that he'd ruin this again, that he'd ruined *her* irreparably. That she still didn't trust him to be there for her and never would.

"I can't think of anything better than another baby with you," he told her gruffly. He'd never meant anything more. "Another member of this family. Our family. It would be a gift."

And Anais laughed. She tipped back her head to look him in the eye and he knew then. She wasn't afraid of telling him this news, she wasn't worried about their future—she was teasing him. She trusted him.

She trusted him.

He couldn't think of a better gift than that.

"Twins," she said, her dark eyes laughing at him. "And get ready, Dare. They're girls."

He couldn't think of a better gift except that, he amended as he covered Anais's mouth with his, love and laughter and that same old hunger underneath, making it all sing.

Except that.

* * * * *

If you enjoyed this book,
look out for the next installment of
THE BILLIONAIRE'S LEGACY:
DI SIONE'S VIRGIN MISTRESS
by Sharon Kendrick.
Coming next month.

MILLS & BOON®
Large Print – February 2017

The Return of the Di Sione Wife
Caitlin Crews

Baby of His Revenge
Jennie Lucas

The Spaniard's Pregnant Bride
Maisey Yates

A Cinderella for the Greek
Julia James

Married for the Tycoon's Empire
Abby Green

Indebted to Moreno
Kate Walker

A Deal with Alejandro
Maya Blake

A Mistletoe Kiss with the Boss
Susan Meier

A Countess for Christmas
Christy McKellen

Her Festive Baby Bombshell
Jennifer Faye

The Unexpected Holiday Gift
Sophie Pembroke

0117 Rom LP